The CURSE *of* CUR

The Chained Gods Series Book 2

Tamira Thayne

WHO Chains YOU PUBLISHING

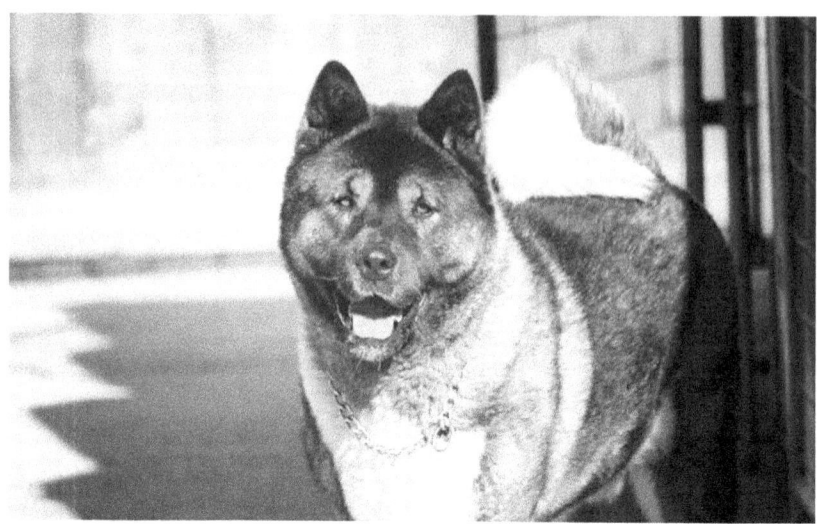

Sprinkles (yes, he is a male) is a gorgeous Akita, and the inspiration for Curjan's dog form. Photo courtesy of JoAnn Dimon, Big East Akita Rescue. B.E.A.R. is a 501(c)3 nonprofit, hands-on, Akita rescue group covering the NY, NJ, and PA metropolitan regions and the Northeast. The group rescues unwanted, abused, and neglected Akitas in need. This gorgeous boy was rescued from the Portage Ohio Animal Shelter. Learn more or donate at bigeastakitarescue.org.

Published by Who Chains You Publishing
P.O. Box 581
Amissville, VA 20106
www.WhoChainsYou.com

Cover Model: Brynakha Vaettir
Cover and interior design: Tamira Thayne
Author website: tamirathayne.com

ISBN-13: 978-1-946044-54-9

Printed in the United States of America

First Edition

To my cat, Charlie Tuna.
They think you can't read,
but maybe they're wrong.

Also by Tamira Thayne

AUTHOR OF
The Wrath of Dog: The Chained Gods Series Book 1

The King's Tether: A Chained Gods Series Prequel Story

The Knight's Chain: A Chained Gods Series Story, Vol. 1.5

Foster Doggie Insanity: Tips and Tales to
Keep your Kool as a Doggie Foster Parent

Capitol in Chains: 54 Days of the Doghouse Blues

The Animal Protector Series:
Smidgey Pidgey's Predicament
Spittin' Kitten's Speed-Away
Raffy Calfy's Rescue

EDITOR OF
More Rescue Smiles: Best-Loved Animal Tales
of Resilience & Redemption

CO-EDITOR OF
Unchain My Heart: Dogs Deserve Better Rescue Stories
of Courage, Compassion, and Caring

Rescue Smiles: Favorite Animal Stories of Love and Liberation

Note from the Author:

The Curse of Cur *is Book 2 of The Chained Gods Series. If you haven't yet read* The Wrath of Dog, *there's a good chance you'll be lost since this book picks up where the first leaves off. Therefore, I highly recommend you read Book 1 first. There are also two optional short stories that flesh out the characters of King Randulf and his second in command:* The King's Tether *and* The Knight's Chain. Happy reading!

Contents

CHAPTER 1: NEW YORK CITY 1

CHAPTER 2: OPEN HEART CHAKRA SURGERY 8

CHAPTER 3: MOMAGEDDON II 13

CHAPTER 4: FLASH MOB 21

CHAPTER 5: TRAIN TRIP 27

CHAPTER 6: JUNKYARD HEAVEN . . .OR WAS IT HELL 33

CHAPTER 7: FANCY MEETING YOU HERE 36

CHAPTER 8: ANYONE SEEN A KEY? 45

CHAPTER 9: FOOD, FUN, FROLIC, AND FROTH 53

CHAPTER 10: DOWN TO BEESWAX 58

CHAPTER 11: AUTO SALVAGE, OR AUTO SAVAGE? 66

CHAPTER 12: MURDER, MAYHEM, MYSTERY, AND
MEMORABILIA 71

Chapter 13: Momma Bear 77

Chapter 14: Hiding and Hunkering.....................87

Chapter 15: Country Living=Da Bomb 96

Chapter 16: Training Day.....................................104

Chapter 17: Downright Right...................................117

Chapter 18: First Christmas 123

Chapter 19: Whip 'Em Good 126

Chapter 20: Speaking of Entanglements.................135

Chapter 21: Uninvited Guest 142

Chapter 22: Christmas Cheer 150

Chapter 23: Ransacking Goes Both Ways...............158

Chapter 24: Video Evidence......................................163

Chapter 25: NYC, Take Two....................................168

Chapter 26: Yeah, Now What?..................................176

Chapter 27: Those Durn Keys....................................180

Chapter 28: Second Dates 185

Chapter 29: The Move at the Movies.....................190

Epilogue: Perrin 194

About the Author.......................................197

CHAPTER 1: NEW YORK CITY

I jumped out of bed, momentarily forgetting about my father slumbering in the chair next to me. My heart gave a tug at his presence, but this was no time for sentimentality. Unbidden, the words *I love you, Dad* whispered through my mind.

Fine, then, maybe just one second for schmaltz.

I couldn't afford to be sidetracked from my vision, I reminded myself—the vision that told me we needed to get to New York City, and fast.

Because I knew where the Akita we'd seen on screen yesterday, my father's second in command, was chained.

My mother is gonna flip her lid.

Mom hated cities in general, declaring them "the 2Ds"—dirty and dangerous—and to her, New York was not just any city, but THE city. THE TERRIFYING ONE.

I wasn't much of a fan either . . . not that I'd ever been there, so really, who was I to be all judgy-judgy. New York City always comes off scary in the movies and TV shows, and between that and my mom's prejudice, I was onboard with any plans that boasted a NYC boycott.

Mom and I were similar in many ways, but whether that was due to nature or nurture, I couldn't say. We were both country girls at heart, even as we currently made our home in the small Virginia town of Culpeper, population 18,227, thank you very much. Our burg flaunted a four-screen movie theatre, a cutesy downtown shopping area complete with its own la-di-da French chocolate shop, and a host of local restaurants to choose from, including a recent addition of the Indian food variety. Yum.

The closest thing I'd seen to a gang in my town was the roving band of Pokemon Go players running amok and raiding virtual gyms on street corners, at landmarks, and in parks. I knew, because Mom and I had joined the Pokemon Go "gang" as our mother-daughter activity last year, hooking up with these marauders of mayhem and discovering the best places in town to catch the imaginary creatures.

I'd quickly gotten bored and moved along, but Mom could occasionally still be seen hanging with her PoGo friends, getting yelled at to "get a life" by irate shopkeepers, and bragging about the legendary "mons" she'd caught. Soon she was carrying her old phone and hotspotting into my account too, playing the game with what she termed her "virtual daughter."

She also claimed her virtual daughter was nicer than me. *Whatevs, Mom.*

Now that I thought about it, I was vastly underprepared to take on the streets of New York City.

As lovers of crisp country air and open skies, Mom and I still held tight to those dreams of a rural home, babbling on about the beauty and peacefulness of our fantasy retreat in the woods, our own kayakable river rambling along mere yards away from our back deck.

There we would open our own animal sanctuary, where

we'd spend all day loving on both our pets and the other critters we saved from certain death, while—in our imaginations at least—someone else did all the hard work of cleaning up and raising money. Yep, that was heaven.

Those dreams were far from my current reality.

Reality told me that my father's (aka King Randulf's) top warrior was chained in dog form (don't ask) at a junkyard in New York City, and he needed us to come and yank him out of that mess. Ten to one he'd been left there to guard the second key to the destruction of two dimensions—Earth and Perrin—too.

Mwahahaha.

My father, who we'd released mere days ago from his own 18-year captivity as a chained German shepherd, was heartbroken over the conditions his warriors still endured, and knowing they were being tortured and starved for decisions he'd made was almost more than he could bear.

But it was time for all of us to buck up. It was my mission, our collective mission, to find his chained warriors, unearth the remaining four keys, and rescue both Perrin and Earth from the grip of Phoebus, The Scion, and their legion of minions.

Easy peasy.

I leaned heavily against the bathroom wall, toothbrush hanging from my mouth.

Oh, who was I kidding.

The future looked daunting, indeed.

I flashed downstairs, eager to talk to Charlie and the

gang about my vision and get their ideas and perspective. I felt a sense of urgency deep in my gut, and knew we needed to find a way to New York City sooner rather than later.

But, as a pseudo-adult who was new to the world of intrigue we'd landed ourselves in, I was more than likely prone to going off half-cocked, and nobody wanted that. *Ha, a little wiener humor.*

Plus, I really didn't know how to explain why I'd had the vision. Was this a new gift? I needed to find Ruth, who worked with auras and could help me clarify what had happened. My best guess was that my fourth chakra "blossomed" the moment I got an eyeful of the Akita on the chain.

I tried to remember the details. I'd felt the familiar "whoosh" up the spine, same as when my solar plexus chakra opened. This time, though, that sensation had left me with such a connection to the Akita that I'd blacked out, and when I awoke later in my room, clearly envisioned where he was and what was happening to him.

It wasn't pretty. He and his retriever companion were chained and in similar dire circumstances to what my father had survived. This vision led to my brilliant analysis that they were also guarding another of the five keys to the super-secret-bad-guy-mind-control-tether machine. *Gulp.*

But we couldn't allow these superfreaks to destroy Perrin and enslave Earth—so we needed to get there, rescue the guy and girl (or doggie and doggette, as the case may be), and grab that key.

Charlie and my mom were deep in discussion in the corner of the living room, as per usual. If she weren't so in love with my father, I'd wonder about her and Charlie, but perhaps they just had a connection that I couldn't yet understand or categorize.

Besides, he's gay after all.

"I heard that," his voice came into my head. "And for the zillionth time, I'm not gay. I know you enjoy pushing my buttons, young lady, but this little joke has gone far enough. Say I'm gay all you want, but I'm not responding anymore. Er, after this time, of course." He appeared a little flustered, gave me a wounded kitten look, and went back to his conversation with my mother.

Speaking of the devil, Momsky was eyeing me in a way I didn't like from across the room.

"What?" I asked defensively.

The gang perked up and began milling about, sensing something was about to go down. I mentally pictured them lining up with their popcorn and sodas.

The Mominator eyed me again. "I know when you're hiding something from me, and you have that look about you. Spill it."

Uh oh. Here goes. And me without backup. I looked around the room, hoping my father had instantaneously appeared. No such luck.

I tried and failed to keep my excitement to myself. "I know where the Akita's chained, Mom! We have to flash to New York City ASAP; he's imprisoned with a golden retriever in some sort of junkyard, and they're both starved and dehydrated the way Dad, Krupert, and Merle were. I'll bet the two dogs are guarding the second key, and now that we're in possession of the first one, what if the bad guys wise up and start moving the others?"

I was beginning to panic now, afraid we were going to lose our shot at getting our hands on that key and saving dad's pack members because my mom had her panties in a wad. Seriously. *It's embarrassing.*

"Did you say New York?" Her voice elevated. *Here we go.* "You know I hate that city more than any other place in this world! I shudder to think of us going there, the dangers we would be exposed to. It's sinister enough as it is, what do you think will happen when we confront these volatile ninjas in a place like that?"

"I know what will happen . . . we'll save the day and win the prize." I said confidently, although truth-be-told I wasn't anywhere near that assured deep down in my quivering, cowardice-filled belly. I couldn't let my mom get a whiff of that, though, so I squared my shoulders and looked her in the eye, hoping my nerves weren't peeking through my facade.

If I can't take on my mom, I'm so screwed when I get to The Scion.

Just then Dad meandered downstairs, still rubbing his eyes. "What's all the yelling about?" he asked innocently.

Now I all but whined, in the way of teenage girls the world over. "Dad, I know where we need to go, but Mom hates New York, so she's throwing a fit about it. Tell her we have no choice; oh, and we have to hurry."

"OK, ok, slow down, honey. I'm still half asleep, and I need to get my wits about me before we get too carried away."

Ruth broke in at that point. "Um, Baylee, I hate to say this, but I can see that your heart chakra has burst open, and your energy field is a roiling mess. I know you don't want a repeat of what happened last time, but I'm afraid there's no way around it. We need to get you upstairs, get that chakra linked up with your others, and see what your newest abilities are."

I grumbled "Fine," pointing my finger from Mom to Dad. "But we're going. So have a little talk, do whatever you grownups do in these situations, and work it out so that we can leave ASAP. As in today. I'll be back downstairs soon."

Ruth and I flashed upstairs to my room, and I was relieved to see that it was just the two of us this time. Mere days ago I'd had to strip down to my birthday suit in front of Ruth, Rebecca, and Tara, but I guess I was old news by now. *Thank Dog.* I'd get to reveal my oh-so-lily-white behind to just one of them.

Ruth stood, arms akimbo. "You know what to do. Lose the clothes. I know it makes you uncomfortable, and I'm sorry we have to do this, but the fabrics here in your land are so nonbreathable; I have a hard time seeing your aura through them. And I most definitely can't do the deep energy work I need to do to link your chakras and bring the newly-opened heart center in line with the others. Rest assured, on Perrin clothing is seen as optional. It's nothing I haven't seen literally millions of times."

That helped. *Not. Because we ain't in Perrin, now is we?*

Chapter 2:
Open Heart Chakra Surgery

I ditched the attire, and Ruth went to work. Even though it was less awkward than the first time, I again stood as dorkily as you can imagine a 17-(and a half)-year-old virgin would stand—in the buff—while being openly analyzed by an energy worker. I gazed about the room, avoided looking at Ruth, and nervously plucked at my hangnails. Bit my lip.

I mean, I suppose I wasn't completely hideous to look at, but still. I was comparatively tall at 5'8", and had always been on the thin side. I had more of a tomboy vibe, as long as said tomboy wasn't actually that great at sports, of course. I ran my fingers awkwardly through my dun-colored mane, studying the ends.

Ruth stepped back, assessing, and frowned as she perused my color scheme and plotted her first move. I could now sense the general blueprint of someone's aura, but Ruth was an expert, and she understood and saw a lot more than I did.

"Stop fidgeting," she ordered. I stood stock still, hating my life.

"Ah HA," she exclaimed. "I know exactly what happened!"

She eyed me critically, and asked the 40-million dollar question that I'd hoped no one would plumb from the recesses of my dense gray matter. "Did you happen to see your mate on that screen yesterday? It's the only explanation that could account for what I'm seeing here. Your heart chakra has blown open, without warning, and flooded the rest of your system. It hasn't linked up to the below chakras as much as overwhelmed them with a massive energy output.

"The heart chakra exudes a green—and loving—vibe, and if you can't see it on yourself, right now your aura is overwhelmingly shamrock. We need to fix that, put it back in balance. Your higher chakras aren't yet open, so we won't worry about them, but that green needs to play nicely with the colors below."

She dove in, deftly using her hands to move the energy and connect it from my heart to my solar plexus, which had opened only days ago, and then on down to my lower root chakras. The sensation was not a pleasant one, and my energy seemed to resist her efforts, fighting back by wending its way about my body, leaving me feeling like I was being tickled by 1000 sadistic pixies. *Awkward.*

Heart chakra!

Dammit. Are rainbows and unicorns about to burst forth from my chest and shower all those in my vicinity with enchanted posies? I didn't want to even think about something so embarrassing. *Love. Bah.*

Ruth continued to prod me for information as she worked.

"Well, did you see your mate? I'm right, aren't I?"

I hung my head. "It wasn't deliberate, I assure you. I

was merely watching the action unfold on the screen like everyone else, when suddenly I felt myself connect up to the Akita, the word 'mate' flashed through my mind, and then everything went black. When I came to, I was relieved to find myself in my own bed, but then I was quickly overtaken by a vision of where he was and an urgent need to go to him. Is this normal? Or am I even more of a freak than everyone thought?"

I was scared, admittedly. I didn't know or understand what was happening to me. I wasn't even an adult yet . . . how could I possibly have a mate?

I had no interest in a life partner; I wanted to flirt with (and maybe kiss) Matt and perhaps a few other handsome lads before even thinking of anything so life-altering as a significant other. *Shudder. WTH.*

Seriously. What in fire and brimstone is going on here?

Ruth started giggling, almost a girlie giggle, which I never would have pegged her for. She ran her fingers through her spikey, multi-hued locks. "Oh, my . . . you bonded with Cur-jan? You are in for it, girl. I can't wait to sit back with some popcorn and a soda and watch the show."

Why am I suddenly the sole source of entertainment for these people? Geez. Get a life.

She messed about in my aura a bit more, then proclaimed me all fixed up and asked how I felt.

I took the opportunity to jump back into my clothes while I thought about it.

"Hmmm," I pondered. "I definitely feel more 'together'. Like my system's back in sync. But now my chest area feels expanded and open, and I kinda don't like it. I feel vulnerable, exposed, like I need to shut down to protect myself.

Does that make any sense?"

"Yes!" Ruth was excited now. "That's exactly it, and why most people close off their heart chakras after they've been hurt emotionally. This occurs even on Perrin, where we're ostensibly more enlightened—although with everything that's happening, our 'enlightened status' is highly questionable at this point.

"There's an innate need to protect ourselves from the pain of loving and feeling rejected; when that hurt comes, people instinctively close off energy to the heart. Yours has probably been shuttered since you were little, because you believed your father abandoned you and your mom, and I'd imagine this left you feeling unloved and unwanted."

A runaway tear dribbled into the crevice along the side of my nose. I noisily brushed it away.

"Argh, now what's happening to me! I'm crying? Is this because you opened my heart? Shut it down!" I shouted, only half joking. I was kinda freaking out, man.

Ruth smiled and squeezed my arm, and for the first time I felt a genuine wave of something akin to affection from her. She'd been pretty standoffish with me from the get-go, and it had gotten even worse when she'd fixed my chakras that first time and I'd inadvertently mindlinked to her. She didn't like that one bit . . . I briefly wondered again if she had something to hide or was just protective of her thoughts.

My own thoughts were in turmoil just now, or perhaps it was this flood of emotion that felt so unfamiliar. Now that my heart chakra had opened, I supposed I'd have to keep it that way so that I could use the gifts it brought, whatever they may be. I wasn't looking forward to it.

"Ruth," I asked, feeling a little shy. "Do you have any idea what gifts come with this? Was my vision of the Akita, er, Curjan you said, part of those abilities?"

Ruth took her healing talk seriously. "It remains to be seen, but the heart chakra normally brings love to the world, and an ability to heal through that flow of love. Since you are unique in that you're half human—yet one of the most powerful Perrinites we've seen—I too am curious as to what abilities you'll glean from this opening.

"Most on our dimension have an innate ability to heal quickly from physical wounds that aren't fatal, so I'm not sure what avenue of healing would manifest for you. I do energy work, also springing from the heart chakra, which heals the aura and brings the body and spirit into alignment, so maybe you'll be gifted with something similar. I'm excited to see where this new path takes you. You're just too unusual for me to predict."

Lucky me.

I gave Ruth a quick hug, and thanked her for helping me. I was genuinely appreciative of all she'd done. I don't know what would have become of me without her here, what with my chakras blowing up all over the place and energy zapping everyone around me. *Lordy, Lordy.*

When I stepped back, Ruth's eyes had teared up, and she looked embarrassed and horrified. "I don't know what's wrong with me today, either," she said. "I NEVER cry! I think your damn chakra is getting to me, too. Yuk. Let's go back downstairs."

We flashed to the living room, just in time to see that an unholy storm had brewed up between Mom and Dad while we were gone.

Yikes! Run...

Chapter 3: Momageddon II

It was Momageddon II! Maybe my father had forgotten, or maybe he'd never faced off with my mom when she was REALLY mad. But I was worried for his safety.

Dad, aka King Randulf, was still chained down the block from us in his German shepherd form when Mom attempted to take down Charlie's crew with her pepper spray, mistakenly believing they were holding me hostage. I snorted at the memory. *That will never get old.*

Mom was nothing if not protective of her little girl. I realized that all her anger, her bluster, was out of love for me and fear for my safety. *I guess opening my heart opened my eyes in some ways, too*, I mused.

I looked over at my mom, and dognabbit if my heart didn't literally start pouring love in her general direction. *Aw, hells.* I could see the green energy wave as it emanated from my chest and wended its way across the room to my mother. Apparently it was visible to some of the others too, because Ruth, Rebecca, Charlie, and my father stopped and stared, mouths agape.

I was a fawn in headlights, not knowing what to do or how to turn off this "faucet of love". When the green wave hit my mother she collapsed to the ground in tears, begging

THE CURSE OF CUR

my father to keep me safe. She'd gone from yelling to crying in a split second, and everyone in the room became flustered and confused at the spectacle created by my family.

They mustn't have Jerry Springer on their dimension.

I smirked.

Obviously, my heart "powers" involved copious amounts of waterworks. Now, to find a way to weaponize that . . . I could picture it now: I go into battle against a batshize truck-load of ninjas, only to send them a big wave of love dust and they all fall like dominos into a blubberfest, apologizing for their evil ways and promising to change.

Actually, I like it. Maybe this heart thing will be useful after all.

Dad dropped to the floor beside mom, who reluctantly allowed him to pull her into his arms. She sobbed quietly, her shoulders rising and falling with each ragged breath. I could hear Dad whispering soothingly into her ear, and I suspected he was sneaking a touch of mindgrind into the mix, too.

I needed that power. An ability to calm down a freaked-out mother? A really necessary gift to have. Maybe it will come with a higher chakra . . . right now my "cry-like-a-baby" power seemed to be taking center stage.

To give Mom and Dad a little privacy, the rest of us sidled our way into the kitchen, cramming ourselves into a space that was not meant for this many people.

Charlie popped into my head. "Care to explain?"

I gave the group, which consisted of Charlie and his nine teammates, plus our new friends Krupert and Merle and mom's best friend Janie, a short rundown of what happened upstairs with Ruth and me, as well as what we surmised took place in the bunker.

Some nodded their heads knowingly, having already thrown out theories amongst themselves, and some stared in amazement. Matt, my crush du jour, was the first to speak. "So you're telling me that Curjan is your MATE? What about you and me? You know nothing about him, the guy's a stuck-up douchebag, and…well, this is just great." He huffed off, flashing himself outside to walk off some of his angst.

Oh, snotgoblins. Matt and I weren't even an item yet, and already I was cheating on him. And apparently with a douchebag. *Ha.*

Charlie, always the voice of reason, cleared his throat. "Excellent detective work, Baylee. Well, then, this is new and surprising information for the group to digest. Whether Curjan and Baylee end up being mates or not is beside the point at this stage of our engagement with the enemy. We've got the well-being of two worlds to consider, which takes precedence over all romantic interludes, I should say. So, Baylee believes the dogs are chained at a junkyard in New York City. Who's been there? Anyone?"

Since Perrinites were forbidden to visit Earth due to the prophecy, and most of these folks were only here to find me, it made sense that the Big Apple had not yet been graced with their presence.

Charlie continued, "No one, then? New York City was on my team's search agenda, Baylee, but we were in Washington, D.C. when we got your coordinates, so we flashed ourselves here instead. Let's ascertain who goes to New York, and who stays here to protect Candice, Janie, the animals, and the property."

Mom's voice rang out from the living room. "I'm going with you. If Baylee goes, I go."

Charlie and Dad both popped into my head, Dad speaking through our mindlink first. "Baylee, honey, your mom can't go to New York. We can't possibly protect her there. Remember what happened in the basement of that house just yesterday? Imagine her in a situation like that. She'd be killed, and she's the glue that holds our little family together. Do you agree?"

I nodded my head. I didn't want Mom anywhere near that fight, Mominator or not. Immortals go down in these battles . . . a human wouldn't stand a chance.

"Charlie, maybe she'll take it better from you. Can you explain the situation to her?"

He ruefully shook his head. "That's what we've been discussing all morning, even before we knew Curjan had been located. She wants to be knee deep in this battle, and won't listen to me when I tell her it's too dangerous for her. I don't know what to do, except trick her, and she'll be exceedingly angry when she finds out."

I looked at Dad, and he at me, and an unspoken agreement formed between us— one of desperation and love. I sent my response through the link to both of them. "Knock her out it is. We'll have to take our punishment when we get back, but at least she'll be alive to kill us."

It was decided that we'd fortify ourselves with breakfast, making false plans which would include Mom and Janie, then Charlie would take them to the couch to "go over a few things with them". There, he'd hit them with a mindbind, putting them into a deep sleep for hours. *God help us.*

Charlie jumped into the minds of his team, relaying the

plan, and King Randulf popped into the heads of Merle and Krupert to do the same.

Tara and Bradley loved to cook, so they got to work in the kitchen whipping up pancakes for 15, while the rest of us pitched in making coffee, fruit salad, and potato wedges.

I made sure to sit next to Mom while we ate, hugging her on occasion and giving her one of my best smiles. She tearfully stared back at me, as if she knew what we were planning, and was trying to let me go without a fight. Maybe I was just being paranoid.

I felt horrible having to trick my own mother, and I knew she'd feel betrayed and terrified for both me and my father . . . for the whole team, really, when she woke up. My mom was caring to a fault, which often got her into trouble, and every single one of the folks here had already been taken under her wing and made part of her family. I knew her well enough to know that.

I imagined she was feeling helpless without any powers or abilities to survive a fight with a Perrinite intent on doing her harm. She was probably in a lonely place, emotionally, right now.

Argh. Heart chakra. There I went again, pondering mushy stuff that just wasn't me. My preference was to ignore all emotions whenever possible, and now the damn things were gushing out of me and spilling onto all unfortunate passersby.

The breakfast table was quieter than usual, what with the team suffering guilt pangs over tricking Mom and Janie, Matt throwing shade in my direction over an unsolicited bond with a dog I'd never met, and a general angst over what we would soon face in New York City.

The silence became oppressive, and Matt jumped up to clear away the dishes. I'd have moved to help, but he seemed in no mood for my company, so I focused on Mom, asking if she'd be missing work by going with us today.

"Janie and I both took two days off, and I shifted my meetings and schedule around so we'll be back in time for me to catch up. I hope," she told me, her voice reflecting her tenuous belief in our ability to free the dogs and get back here quickly.

Janie was as loyal to my mom as a best friend could be, and had received special privileges like being indoctrinated into the gang as a result; admittedly, although I loved Janie like a second mother, I was still a little salty about it.

My best friend, Amaya, had not been given the green light to join the group by Charlie and my father, and it had driven a wedge as big as my bicep between she and I. I'd been forced to blow her off repeatedly, making up lies to cover the truth she wasn't allowed to know, and now she wouldn't even talk to me.

It hurts, I acknowledged, if only to myself. When and how could I to make it up to her, especially if I wasn't "allowed" to bring her into the mix?

I resolved that if we made it back from New York safely—with the new warriors and the second key—I was sitting her down and telling her everything. Screw it. If I'm to be savior of two dimensions, then I too deserve to have my best friend at my side, helping me through it the way Mom had Janie.

I straightened my chin and stood. It felt good to take back some form of control over my life.

I carried plates to the sink, where Matt and his twin Jake were doing the dishes and filling the dishwasher. Jake gave me a warning look that said "Beat it, Bay," so I held up my hands in defeat, retreating upstairs to care for my kitties.

At least they want me around . . .

I dropped into the bean bag chair I kept in our cat room and immediately found myself smothered in kitty lovins', just the way I liked it. BooBoo, Una, and Tootie all clamored for attention, climbing into my lap and snuggling in.

"I can only stay a few minutes, guys," I told them. "Then I have to go rescue my mate, who probably eats sweet little kitties like you all for breakfast. Don't worry, though, no one's gonna tell ME who I have to be with, and I have no intention of leaving my babies for an Akita. Yuck."

I burrowed my face into Una's fur, while BooBoo kneaded on my stomach and Tootie rubbed her face into my hand. *Ah, now if this isn't a little slice of fur-bearing heaven.*

I stayed like that for a good five minutes, just soaking up the love of those who'd been my support system for as long as I could remember. With every cell in my body, I wanted to avoid what my life had become—avoid the unknown terrors I was about to face, avoid making decisions and mistakes that could doom not only my team but the planet as well.

I reluctantly pushed the kitties aside and scooped the poop, topped off the dry food bowl, and cleaned their water dispensers. Then I gave the room a quick run-through with our "made for pets" vacuum cleaner and looked around in satisfaction.

At least when Mom wakes this will be one thing off her plate, and one less reason to want my head.

I flashed back downstairs to see that Mom and Janie were already out, and Dad had carried mom up to bed. Smith picked Janie up, asking Ruth where to put her. Ruth brushed

Janie's cheek with her hand, and a small smile lit her face. *Ha, I knew there was something going on there . . . have to do some digging . . .*

"Go ahead and flash her to the same bed as Candice," said Dad. "That way when they wake up, they'll at least be together and can get started on their plot for retribution right away." A wan smiled tugged at his mouth, although it didn't reach his eyes.

Smith nodded, flashed away with Janie, and was back in less than 3 seconds.

I guess that means it's time to go. Ugh.

I felt sick to my stomach.

CHAPTER 4: FLASH MOB

D aniel, Charlie's second in command and the battle strategist of the group, stepped forward now that the REAL planning could begin. Deep in thought, he pushed his fingers through his red hair before seeming to come to a decision. "Without Perrin's special flash tunnels at our disposal, we have to think first about how we get to New York the fastest. Here's what I propose. We can flash as a group about 100 miles away, tops, without needing a rest. Since some of us flash better than others, I recommend that Smith, Charlie, and King Randulf take a small group each— they're our most gifted and can more readily carry the load, so to speak."

He continued. "Baltimore is about 100 miles from here as the crow flies. We'll get the coordinates for the train station and flash there, catching the next train to Philadelphia. They run all hours of the day. Then from Philadelphia it's another 100 miles to New York City; at that point we'll be rested and can flash the rest of the way. How does that sound?"

Krupert, our new friend and the leader of the Perrinite rat sect spoke up. "What role shall Merle and I play? Should we stay here to protect Candice and ensure all is well on this end while you're gone?"

The King gave a relieved sigh. "Yes, thank you! Great idea, Krupert. That's actually what I was hoping for as well, but I worried you'd want to be part of the fight. With you and Merle still regaining your strength from your kidnapping ordeal, perhaps this will be better all the way around. Do you think you can handle Candice when she wakes up, though? She's going to be a bit on the feisty side."

Krupert grinned, while Merle had the good sense to look afraid. *Smart man.* "I've got a like-minded woman of my own at home, so I'm used to talking a woman down from the roof when need be. I believe you and I will have a strong enough mindlink connection even from 300 miles away, so I'll be able to assure her all is well with you, and vice versa. Plus, if there's one thing Merle and I specialize in, it's finding hidden ways in and out of places. We'll spend the next few hours devising a plan to evacuate the house and move everyone to safety in case any ninjas come our way."

Daniel, satisfied with Krupert's strategy and abilities, moved on with our plan. "Baylee, have you had any more visions that might tell us in which junkyard the dogs are chained? I feel confident we can be in New York in a matter of hours, but I'm at a loss as to how to locate them once we hit the city. While we're on the train I'll work with Curtis and Jake to spotlight all the junkyards. Then we'll bring the info to you and see if anything strikes a chord. Sound alright?"

Everyone nodded, and we broke for a few minutes while we took bathroom breaks and suited up. We couldn't drag any noticeable weapons through the streets of Baltimore, Philly, or New York, but Smith grabbed a small tool case and ensured he had his trusty drill—which had come in handy against the pythons—and a few other necessary items for breaking and entering or other emergency situations.

Back downstairs, the mood was both charged and subdued, with folks amping up for a fight but feeling ill-equipped to take on the magnitude of the task we'd set for ourselves. I knew the feeling. Minus Mom, Janie, Krupert, and Merle, we numbered eleven. We split into two teams of four and one of three, and I found myself grouped with Dad and Ruth, who seemed to be gravitating to my side now that we'd had our weird bonding moment upstairs.

Before we left I embraced both Krupert and Merle, asking them to protect Mom and my critters with their lives. After they'd assured me they would, Daniel gave the "all clear", and I was immediately overtaken by the rush of the long-distance flash. *Holy furballs! What a bizarre feeling!*

The furthest I'd flashed, before this moment, was the house two blocks away where we'd discovered the chained German shepherd dubbed Wrath, aka King Randulf, aka Dad. I'd felt next to nothing when doing so—a simple wish to be over there, throw out a quick mind tether to where I wanted to land, and whoosh, I was there.

But flashing 100 miles away? That, I was not prepared for.

Dad threw out his mental tether to the coordinates Daniel gave him, and then, because it was so far, I had time to actually experience the reality of travel by mind tether. It was as if we'd somehow created our own invisible tunnels, with Dad grasping both Ruth and I by the arm to ensure we stuck together. I would have expected to feel nauseous, but even though I felt the rush through time and space, there was no sickness. *Perrin genes, I guess.*

We all landed as a group, smack dab in the middle of

the crowded train station. In a stroke of bad luck, we'd also landed in a fruit vendor's stall, with Daniel, Matt, Jake, and Curtis toppling into a heap amidst a crate of now-mangled watermelons. The fruit vendor, who appeared to be of Chinese descent, awoke from a nap and looked about him with wide-eyed astonishment. He wagged his finger at us, yelling in broken English. "You pay! You pay all. You ruin watermelon, pay $100 dollars now! I call police."

Realizing that a scene was the last thing we needed, I jumped forward, holding out my hands in what I hoped was a soothingly submissive gesture.

"Sir, it's ok. We'll pay for everything. So sorry. How did this happen?" I faked confusion, looking around like I had no idea how we ended up here either. "One second, sir."

Daniel and the guys, chagrined, had pulled themselves out of the bin, watermelon juice and pulp dripping from their clothing. I grabbed Daniel and pulled him aside, absently plucking a seed from his red hair. "You've gotta flash back to change anyway, right? I need you to get in Mom's drawer in her room and pull out some cash. I completely forgot this is the real world, and we'll need money for train tickets, too. Now we gotta pay this guy. Grab $500 of her emergency stash, and I'll explain it to her later."

I turned to the others. "Looks like you need to go change, too, but hurry. And flash back into that hallway over there, so no one sees you next time. We'll have to mindgrind everyone here, make them forget they saw us or make them think they saw something else. I need that $100 ASAP for this guy, though, before he calls the cops."

Matt, still with an obvious chip on his shoulder about Curjan and I, snarled. "Why don't you just mindgrind him too, Baylee, so he doesn't call the cops and then we wouldn't even have to pay him?"

Oh. This is not an attractive look on him, I snarked to myself.

I felt my face flame at his reminder of my "newby-status", anger and embarrassment grappling for top spot. I deflected, returning his snotty words with some snark of my own. "No need to be a butt, Matt. Yeah, I get it. I'm new to this world, and can't even mindgrind on my own yet, so I'm not that great at putting our gifts to use. Regardless, we should pay the man his money anyway, since we DID ruin his fruit."

Daniel grabbed Matt before our brawl could escalate, and flashed the four of them home. Charlie and Dad were busy creating a diversion on the other side of the food court by "encouraging" two vendors to start yelling at each other. The few folks that didn't fall for the distraction were hit with a mild mindunwind, just enough to cause confusion and help them forget the last few minutes ever happened.

Satisfied with their work, the men turned to me. I was deep in talks with the fruit vendor, practicing my own mindgrind as I threw a mental tether his way and sent some calming vibes down its length. It worked—maybe a little too well—since he immediately slumped to the floor, snoring and scratching his butt through his loose pants. *Yikes. TMV. Too Much Visual.*

Daniel and the boys were back within minutes, so we slipped a $100 bill into the sleeping man's hand and Charlie gave him a mental slap to wake him as we took our leave.

The next train was five minutes from departure, so we rushed to the ticket window, bought 11 passes to Philly, and made it to our seats just as the train was pulling out of the station. I sat back, relieved, and Dad plopped down beside me.

I gave him a weary smile, laying my head on his shoulder. I didn't think I'd ever get over having my father back in my life, and I hoped I never stopped appreciating it and him, even through the bad times. Even though all the nasty shize was slapping us silly right now, there was still a part of me that felt like the luckiest girl in the world.

CHAPTER 5: TRAIN TRIP

Inodded off, and was jostled awake at the next station. I leaned back in my seat, surreptitiously wiping my mouth to see if I'd been drooling. *So sexy, Bay.*

I looked over at Dad, and he stared back with a goofy grin on his face.

"What? Do I have booger nose or something?" I ran my finger back and forth across the bottom of my nostrils, just to be sure.

"No, honey, nothing like that. You have no idea how thrilled I am to just be with you right now. I can hardly believe I have a daughter at all, let alone take in the fact that she's practically an adult, and I get the honor of being her father—however late I am to the party." The silly grin remained in place.

"Um, awkward, Dad," I said, secretly pleased. I patted his arm. "I mean, I'm not gonna lie. I'm a teensy bit thrilled to have you around, too. Even though you look young enough to be my brother . . . which is way creepy. When are you gonna do something about that?"

"Oh! I meant to handle that today, actually. I need a few hours of peace and quiet to work with my cells on the aging process. I know it makes your mother uncomfortable, too. I guess it will have to wait until we get back home now, honey. I'm sorry. Rest assured I'll take care of it as soon as I can."

"Thank you, Daddy," I grinned, snuggling into his arm. If anyone noticed us, they'd take us for a young couple in love, but I pushed that disturbing thought out of my brain. I couldn't wait for him to age enough to actually look like my dad.

He moved our conversation to a private, mindlinked "room" with just the two of us in it. There were too many humans around with prying eyes and open ears. Talking about all that was going down with Perrin, Earth, and the evil minions was definitely something that needed to be done on the down low.

"Honey, how are you handling all of this. I know it's been a lot for you to take in on such short notice. You've been thrown into the deep end of the pool, and not only do you not have a life preserver, you're in the middle of a hurricane and gale force winds are pummeling you."

I shrugged. "I think for the most part everything's moving so quickly I haven't had much time or privacy to fall apart. And that's probably a good thing, because I do love a good wallow. I guess I'll just keep muddling along until I have a complete mental breakdown, at which point you'll have to bring in the cavalry to prop me back up again." I gave him a weak smile.

I suddenly remembered what I'd wanted to ask as soon as I woke up, before the vision overtook me and things got crazy again. "Oh!" I exclaimed. "How many ninjas survived last night's battle . . . and where are they?"

Dad looked grimmer than I'd seen him since he came back into his human form. "Three of the five that were in ninja form survived. All four that took python form perished due to Matt and Smith's quick thinking with the drillbit, and, as you know, I took the life of the one that sent me into flashbacks. The man that Daniel fought swallowed a poison tab he'd hidden in a special pocket the second he came to."

He took a deep breath and then continued. "Once we realized they were all carrying suicide packs, we checked the other three and removed their doses without incident. As of right now we have two males and a female in custody. Both of the ninjas you fought survived."

I felt relief mixed with a bit of guilt that I might not have been sad enough if I'd killed them. *What's wrong with you, Baylee? Psychopath much?*

"So where are they now, then? They weren't at the house."

"No, we didn't want to take them there, in case they had tracking implants, which has since been confirmed. Charlie and I called for Perrin's equivalent of your FBI, and they sent an extraction team to pick them up directly from the property. Right now they are safely ensconced at our head-quarters, and will be interrogated starting today." He looked at his watch. "In fact, I'm sure our men and women have been at it all morning. I imagine I'll be hearing from them with an update soon."

I was glad that was at least one thing off my plate, something I didn't need to deal with or worry about. I was nervous about trusting folks I didn't know yet on Perrin, though . . . how many of them, if any, had turned to the dark side? Were the higher echelons infiltrated with traitors? How would we find out?

Even though this was Dad's concern and not mine, I

decided to ask him about it. Naively trusting the folks on his planet had gotten Dad and all the Perrinites into this mess in the first place. If it was my job to get them out, I was going to have to consider everyone I met guilty until proven innocent.

That's what my gut told me, anyway, and I'd decided my gut was smarter than I was.

"So, Dad . . . what makes you believe in the people who came to pick up Phoebus' minions? Shouldn't we be running some kind of lie detector test on all your staff to find out who might be moonlighting as part of the Foul Faction of Nefarious Ninjas?"

Dad's chuckle echoed through my mind. "Foul Faction? Nefarious Ninjas?"

I blushed and lifted my chin. "Yeppah—that's the name I made up for them. What? I'm a nickname giver, and that seems way cooler than calling them Phoebus' minions, or the evil dudes and dudettes. Plus, regular ninjas aren't always creepy, but these guys certainly are. So they needed a special name. We'll call them EfofEn, Foul Faction, or Nefarious Ninjas for short if we want to. There are all kinds of fun nicknames available from that combo.

"And we're the Savage Squad, which, in today's lingo, means we're tough. So you can call them what you will, but those are my names for them."

"Done, Daughter: Foul Faction of Nefarious Ninjas vs. the Savage Squad it is," he smirked, rolling his eyes.

Well, it seemed cooler when I dreamed it up, I acknowledged to myself.

"As for your question, yes, Charlie and I have been discussing it at length. As you know, different folks on our dimension are born with different gifts. Our PBI (Perrinite Bureau of Investigation) employs our most gifted mind-linkers—those like me who can actually slip in through cracks and get around blocks such as those we found in the minds of Krupert and Merle. Many of these traitors could in fact be mindswiped, our term for brainwashed, and if so would not even be aware that they were working for the bad guys. We will bring these folks back to reality if we possibly can, to save their lives."

He paused. "We haven't wanted to cause widespread panic on Perrin, given what we've learned about the depths of the betrayal. We've decided to wait until the investigators are done questioning our prisoners, to see what else may come to light. In the meantime, a team of five men and women with the highest levels of security clearance is handling the initial interrogations. For now, trust Charlie and I, if you can trust anyone. Now that we are aware of the danger surrounding us, we're taking every precaution."

I sighed in relief, dropping that load from my already-sagging shoulders. "Thanks for getting me in the loop, Dad. If I'm to play a major role in the upcoming weeks on both Perrin and Earth, I'd appreciate if I could be kept up to speed on pretty much everything. Don't sugarcoat it or try to protect me. I need to know the same facts you and Charlie are working with, so I can look at it from a fresh perspective and hopefully give some input, too. Deal?"

"Deal, Sweetheart."

We sat back, releasing our mindlink and retreating into our own thoughts for the remaining twenty minutes before we hit Philly. Although I was still worried about everything we faced, I relaxed and watched the scenery splash by my window, making believe I was just an ordinary teen taking a day trip with her dad.

Who knew that would sound like a little slice of raspberry pie utopia about now.

Ah, to be ordinary again.

CHAPTER 6: JUNKYARD HEAVEN . . . OR WAS IT HELL

J ust before we were due to pull into Philly, Daniel plopped down beside me with an exasperated sigh. Yanking out a burner phone he'd acquired at the Baltimore station, he produced a list of almost 120 junkyards in New York City alone.

"Well, Baylee," he started, throwing out a mindlink tether so our conversation wouldn't be overheard. "We've got a problem on our hands. There's no way we can logistically check out all these junkyards in one day, even with our abilities to flash. I hate to split up the team, because we don't know what we're going to encounter, and it's just not safe. Can you look this list over and let me know if you get any visions or tingles about any of these places? If we had five that were on a short-list to visit, we could knock that out in an hour, tops."

He handed me the phone. Without warning, my heart started beating in time with a sudden and overwhelming pounding at my temples. I thought I was gonna pass out. I shoved my fear back into the pit of my stomach—how did *that* escape—along with whatever crazy performance anxiety was taking center stage, and grabbed hold of the device.

I scrolled through the names, feeling nothing at all, until I was about a quarter of the way down the list. Suddenly the name "Big A Auto Salvage" bounced out and hit me between the eyes, and my gut screamed "YES! Yes, Yes!" I panicked and dropped the phone, my eyes widening as my heart skipped a beat or ten.

Daniel plucked the phone from the floor, popping into my head again. "Whoa! What happened?"

"Well," I said sardonically. "Either I found them, or there's a used part I need for my Sexy Saturn at Big A Auto Salvage in Brooklyn. I'm gonna go with the first one."

Daniel's narrowed his eyes. "What did you see?"

"I didn't *see* anything. It was my gut talking to me, which has been very vocal since Ruth got it communicating with the rest of my body. The name literally jumped off the screen at me, then my gut blasted me with a chorus of 'Yesses' . . . about a million of them. Or three."

"That's good enough for me," Daniel said, popping off the chair as we pulled into the station. "Let's gather the troops, and make our way to . . ." He looked at his phone again. ". . . Blecker Street, number 5081 to be exact, Brooklyn." He nodded and started up the aisle, touching the others by the arm as he popped into their heads and gave them the low down. I jumped to my feet and started to follow.

Dad and Charlie both crashed my mind at the same time, scaring me. *How will I ever get used to that? And, get any damn privacy to fall apart as needed?*

"Sorry, Baylee," Charlie said. "We've done it so long that we actually feel when someone's 'ringing the bell'. Hopefully the same will happen for you, so you can stop being frightened and we can stop feeling guilty for alarming you. Well done on picking up the location, by the way. It appears your powers are coming along nicely."

"Thanks, oh favorite gay uncle," I replied blithely, trotting out my overused—and socially unacceptable—joke as revenge for the fright inflicted upon my personage. But, as luck would have it, Charlie had the last laugh after all, because when I turned around to see if I'd managed to irritate him, I full-body slammed into the back of a big biker-type dude waiting his turn to get off the train.

I hurt myself (and my pride) more than I hurt him, because I bounced off his brick wall of a body and would have landed flat on my beehive if my not-so-gay uncle Charlie hadn't caught me. He stood me upright before bursting into laughter, causing Dear Old Dad to crack up at my expense too. *Argh. Men.*

I huffed myself off the train and into the bathroom, where I took a few moments to use the facilities, wash up, and get over myself. Rebecca and Ruth followed me in, Rebecca touching my arm in a silent question.

"Yeppah, I'm ok. Let's get this over with," I said, jumping up and down and shaking out my arms, hoping to get the adrenaline and angst working to wake me up and prepare me for what was to come.

We met the rest of the gang outside and grouped up, seconds from flashing to an unknown fate against a barely known enemy on behalf of a beloved warrior and a potential unwanted mate.

What could possibly go wrong?

CHAPTER 7:
FANCY MEETING YOU HERE

We landed in a heap—fine—*I* landed in a heap, tripping over my own two feet as we whooshed to a stop immediately outside the Big A Auto Salvage that had set off my pinger. Everyone else just watched as I lumbered to my feet, smiling sheepishly and shrugging my shoulders.

"Hey, at least I didn't land on any watermelons," I smirked at Matt, who just eyed me coldly. *Whatevs.*

Daniel, aka our general, herded us behind some honeysuckle bushes to cut down on the odds of us being immediately outed as intruders. We didn't know what kind of security system was in place here, or even if the owners of this fine establishment were in on any dirty deeds that were going down.

Randulf and Charlie formed a mindlink "conference room" that contained everyone in the party, and I had a moment of gift envy. That would come in mighty handy.

Daniel spoke through the grouplink, outlining the plan. "We'll need to flash to the other side of this wall to avoid going through the front door en masse. We don't want to arouse suspicion if we don't have to, but I don't want us splitting up because I have no idea what we're up against. The last thing we need is anyone captured or killed because they don't have backup."

Just then a loud, wailing siren pierced the air, rendering Daniel silent and throwing the place into chaos. We peered through the bushes to see eight ninjas pour out of the building next to us and through the large front gate that was used to bring in wreckers and other trucks towing salvage vehicles.

Um, if they're after us they took a wrong turn . . .

We were on high alert now, everyone's eyes jumping from Daniel to Charlie to King Randulf for guidance.

The King took command. "This is unexpected, but let's use this chaos as cover. They've only posted one sentry by the gate. Daniel, Smith, flash over there and grab that sentry and bring him back here. Let's have us a little pow wow real quick."

Daniel and Smith were two of our most able-bodied warriors, and they easily captured and subdued the EfofEn guard. The man, dressed in their signature black from head to toe and with a black mask covering his face, wasn't unconscious, but he wasn't far from it after the hurtin' Smith had put on him.

He was with it enough to do a double take after seeing the king, at which point the fear on his face was palpable. "K-K-King Randulf! We thought you were dead! Where have you been all these years?"

Taking advantage of the man's obvious deference, Dad paced toward him. "What's your name, Son?"

"Petra, Sir."

"Petra. While I'll be happy to regale you with the details

later, right now we're in a bit of an emergency situation. Can you tell me what's happening here? Why the sirens?"

"I c-c-c-can't, Sir. They'll kill me." He raised a hand to his neck, to the same spot where we'd removed the implant they'd put into Matt when they kidnapped him.

Ah. So the bastages force compliance? Those no-good sumb's . . .

Dad and Charlie were holding a two-man conversation in their heads, I could sense it. I stormed the proverbial mind door. "Excuse me . . . I'm supposed to be part of this stuff from now on, remember?"

"Oh, sorry, Miss Baylee," said Charlie. "We've decided to just knock this guy out for now . . . we don't have time to cajole him or carry him along with us. We don't want to kill those who might be salvageable, and that obviously takes time to figure out. Does that sound agreeable to you?"

I flicked my hand. "Yep, go for it."

Charlie nodded at Daniel, who quickly put the man in a sleeper hold and cradled him as he fell to the ground, throwing in some mindbind once he was out. "That should hold him for at least 30 minutes, enough time to get in and out."

Smith dragged the guy back a little further so he wouldn't be visible, and we flashed to just beyond the door he'd been guarding.

We were met with a view not unlike those you'd see in those post-apocalyptic TV shows that had become so popular.

Everyone plunged into ready stance, but there was no one around to fight. In front of us stood a massive labyrinth of junk cars, some smashed and stacked 50 feet high, with in-between areas resembling a skeletal parking lot, waiting to be picked clean by the vultures of the auto world.

Our eyes roamed the arena, attempting to make sense of the layout and understand why the sirens were still going off. Why weren't we seeing any fleeing people? There were no signs of fire or other natural catastrophes.

We hunkered down, Daniel signaling us to stay low and follow him. We rushed around the first stack of squashed cars and paused—nothing. A roadway wide enough to squeeze a single vehicle ran the next 200 yards, and we stuck to the dim edges, Daniel at the forefront giving updates via mindlink. At the end the road made a sharp right turn, and we stopped in the shadows to regroup.

We could hear a commotion coming from that direction, but the stacks of cars and debris blocked our view. Smith peeked around the corner and frantically turned back, motioning us into the shadows. "The dogs! They're headed this way . . . full steam, probably still feral, and unable to flash or even realize they can flash. Even worse, I'm seeing at least five ninjas hot on their tails! King?"

The king, charged with the ultimate leadership decisions, acted without hesitation—these were his warriors to protect, and he was not about to leave them hanging. "Baylee, Charlie, you two and I will grab the dogs as they run past and then I'll flash us all to an empty lot I can sense two blocks from here. Hopefully with our combined gifts we can bring them around quickly. The rest of you will have to stand and fight as a distraction, then flash in behind us. Got it?"

Everyone nodded, just as Curjan in Akita form and the golden retriever barreled around the corner. The King grabbed Curjan, who thrashed and twisted his head to bite, while Charlie and I double-teamed Samantha, flashing immediately to the vacant property with the dogs. As soon as we landed (yes, I stayed upright, thank you very much), Curjan viciously launched into attack mode, seemingly too feral to comprehend that Randulf was his King and pack leader, not the enemy.

The retriever, Samantha, was light as a feather; her fur was missing in patches, and she stunk to high heaven. My heart broke. It was pitiful that this poor creature was even alive after being starved for so long. Unlike Curjan, she didn't struggle in our arms at all—in fact, she seemed to have given up without a fight, her will to live having been zapped from her for so long that she welcomed death.

Both dogs shook with adrenaline and fear, their eyes glazed, whites readily visible, and pupils dilated. I rushed from Samantha's side to Dad's to help subdue Curjan, who hadn't yet begun to give up his fight for life.

It was obvious that these dogs had been traumatized for years, couldn't yet remember that they were more than wild beasts, or that they were in fact highly-trained warriors of the king who'd saved them.

Curjan lunged, grabbing Dad by the arm, and I reacted without thought, tackling him to the ground and laying on top of him to protect my father. He too was a rack of bones, a wretched creature, but these small facts failed to register on more than a subconscious level.

Because as soon as my touch reached beneath the dog's fur to his skin, a surge of electrical current leapt from me to him, shocking us both and pulling forth a flood of emotions from within me. I jumped away from his body in confusion and fear, worried I'd somehow hurt him further when he couldn't take any more abuse.

But instead of injuring him, our connection immediately transformed him to human form, and he lay there gasping for breath, naked, and quaking.

Dad jumped into action, whipping a pair of sweats and sweatshirt from his backpack and tossing them to Curjan. "Here, Son, put these on. Do you need help? Can you speak?"

Curjan waved him off, refusing to look him in the eye, shame and embarrassment still draped about his skeletal frame. He wordlessly pulled himself off the ground and shakily drew on the pants and shirt.

Oi. So very awkward, with just a touch of hubba. I'm a perv, I sighed.

Averting my eyes, I left him to Dad's capable hands and raced back to the retriever. Just as I reached her the rest of the warriors arrived carrying Rebecca, who was unconscious and sporting a pretty major head wound. Matt was propped between Jake and Curtis, favoring his left foot and still managing to give me baleful looks despite his injury, his eyes flitting back and forth between me and Curjan. *Oh, brother.*

I'd had it. I jumped into his mind, invited or not, and fumed in his general direction. "What the H.E. Double Hockey Sticks is wrong with you? Are you seriously butthurt over me and a guy I never even met before, to the point of screwing up our mission? Get your head on straight, Matt. I'm not planning to MATE with anyone anytime soon. I'm not even an adult yet! And you're letting yourself get so distracted you've put yourself and our whole team in danger. Buck up, Buddy."

His mouth dropped open, and he shoved me out of his

head. At least he had the grace to look chagrined, and there was a lessening of the glare factor in my general direction, so that worked for me.

Now, where was I.

Curjan had himself dressed, and was doing his best to avoid looking at me as he somberly stood beside The King, head hanging. Dad put his arm around Curjan's shoulders and murmured in low tones; I looked away again, perfectly happy to avoid all things Curjan myself. I'm not sure what that whole energy-zapping thing was, but I could spend eternity pretending it never took place as long as everyone else was on board.

Samantha was still in dog form, and Charlie was petting and soothing her in a calm voice. I walked over to the two of them, and he quickly popped into my head. "Baylee, can you bring her around to human form too? She's very shut down, and I'm hoping between the two of us we can help her remember who she is. That is, if you have any energy left after accosting poor Curjan?" He allowed himself a slight quirk to his mouth, and I knew this was his revenge on me for all the gay jokes.

Dognabbit, I should have known there'd be payback sooner or later . . .

I huffed. "I'm fine, Charlie, and Curjan survived my assault, too," I said, defensively.

"I'll just bet he did, now, didn't he," Charlie continued his merciless onslaught.

"Argh! I give . . . you win. No more gay jokes. Happy now? Just tell me what I need to do."

He smiled, patting me on the head. "Good girl. Simply touch her the way you did with my team when we first met and were still in cat form. Aside from your elevated strength, this was your earliest manifested gift. Now that your father is no longer in canine form, his warriors should be able to easily transform back to their immortal forms, too. That's what you just did with Curjan—among other things."

Snicker.

"Hey! I thought we had a deal? You're not gay, and I'm not drooling over Curjan."

Charlie sighed, unhappy that his revenge was coming to such an early end. "I suppose, Miss Baylee. One for the road, that's all. Truce it is…BUT if you go back on your word, I go back on mine as well, and the war of sexual innuendo will continue unabated."

"Done," I muttered, bummed that I'd been outfoxed by a man who turns into a cat.

I plopped onto the ground beside Samantha and put my hand on her skeletal ribcage. She trembled beneath my touch, but this time there was only a slight energy burst, which poured from my hand and encircled her body. Ruth readied a set of clothes for her as I worked, and as soon as Samantha transformed into a beautiful and willowy woman with dark golden hair, Ruth scooped her up and helped her dress, finishing with a brief yet reassuring hug.

Ruth then handed her off to Charlie, "Could you please take over here? I need to get back to Rebecca and see what's wrong with her. Her healing has kicked in, but I think she still needs a little support. Baylee, can you come help me? We all noticed that when you helped us transform, we felt great. I suspect your touch boosts our own healing abilities."

I was dubious, myself. "Sure, if you want, I'll give it a try. But don't expect too much." I walked with her to where

Rebecca lay on the ground, white as a sheet.

Ruth immediately pulled me into a lesson in working with auras. "Can you see how her aura has a slight greenish tint to it?" I nodded. "That's because healing is her strongest gift, and green is the color of the heart chakra and the ability to heal. But look at her head…can you see how it's got a blackish area hovering just above where that cut lies?"

I took a closer look, and nodded, excited. "I see it, I really do!"

Ruth smiled, like I was her pupil and about to collect my first gold star. "In order for me to smooth her healing path, I'll pour some of my own heart chakra energy into her aura, pushing the black and gray away and weaving my own green into her energy field. Watch me, and then try it yourself."

She proceeded to do exactly as she described; it looked easy enough, and I actually felt a little eager to give it a try myself. *Who knew.* I jumped in with her, weaving my own green ooze from my heart chakra into Rebecca's diminished aura spots, delighted when I saw her visible wounds closing up.

Ugh, I hope she doesn't cry when she wakes up.

Within moments, we had succeeded in pushing all the gray from Rebecca's aura. She opened her eyes, took in her surroundings, and promptly burst into tears.

Oh, Good Lord of all cows and chickens. Seriously? I'm getting a complex here!

Ruth wasn't bothered, though, yelling "Yay!" as she hugged her sister.

I had to admit, it did warm the cockles of my heart to see these seemingly no-nonsense sisters care for each other . . . Inside, they were just a coupla' softies after all.

Chapter 8: Anyone Seen a Key?

D ad, Charlie, and Daniel quickly consulted, and we flashed to a hotel on Long Island, well away from the salvage yard we'd just infiltrated, but close enough to come back if need be.

Using my "for-emergencies-only" credit card (Mom was gonna triple kill me), we booked a double suite and got everyone into the rooms so we could aid our two trauma-tized rescuees and plan our next move.

As soon as all 13 of us made it safely inside and Bradley had thrown up a mindchime—aka sound barrier—everyone started talking at once. Charlie's team hadn't "hung out" with Dad's warriors on a frequent basis when they worked for the government in Perrin; but they were friendly and had crossed paths often enough to have built a solid working relationship.

Most on Perrin had believed The King and his warriors were dead; now, Charlie's team was excitedly mobbing Cur-jan and Samantha to welcome them back to the world of the living and find out what they'd been through.

Overwhelmed with it all, Curjan and Samantha sat at the edge of one of the beds, close together, still seemingly dazed.

They looked about the room, studying faces and furnishings, as if they'd never seen any of it before.

I was a little freaked out by their zombiefied behavior.

Dad, as their leader, took control and nudged everyone else away, hunkering in front of them to appear non-threatening and speaking gently. "Curjan, Samantha, it's me, King Randulf. Nod if you can understand me."

They both nodded, but huddled even closer together. I felt a stab of jealousy pierce my heart, which was ridiculous given that I'd never even met the guy before, and still hadn't exchanged so much as a word with him.

I knew nothing about him as a person, other than the memory of that stupid word—*"mate"*—flashing through my head, Ruth giggling about my bond with him, Matt's low opinion of his suitability, oh, and who could forget that brief flash of his junk as he transformed from an Akita into his human-form birthday suit.

There are some things best left to the imagination of a lily-white virgin such as myself. Snort.

I backed up further, trying to blend in with the other peeps squeezed into the living room behind Dad. I was onboard with NOT meeting him, ever, if that were possible, but I knew that was probably wishful thinking.

I mean, don't get me wrong; I was glad he was safe and all, and my overwhelming drive to SAVE HIM was gone, Thank Dogness . . . so now if I could just disappear into the woodwork and call it a day, I'd be down with that.

Wishful thinking aside, I assumed I was gonna have to woman up and deal with him being around, in whatever form that took. *Sigh.*

Dad continued. "Can either of you remember what happened to you . . . how long you've been here. Anything, really?"

Curjan went first. He appeared to be gathering his thoughts, and a frown built between his eyebrows. He slowly stood, but he was wobbly, prompting Bradley to zip downstairs to get them both some water, a coke for a jolt of energy and sugar, and a coupla' sandwiches to eat.

Even though I tried not to really *look* at him, not to see him as a man, I couldn't help but be drawn to him, to study him. As an Akita he had certainly been majestic— despite his skeletal condition—what with his big chocolate eyes, dark brown fur around his face and back, and lighter patches coating the rest of his body.

Yet as a human—er, immortal, whatever—he was just as striking, to my eyes at least. Despite the fact that he still appeared underweight, I could tell he was well-framed and even muscular, as hard as that was to believe. His chocolate eyes met mine, burning into my soul for a second before flitting away, and I wondered if it was my imagination—did he felt the connection between us too?

And wanted it to go away? Yep. Probably.

He was tall, probably 6'2", with shaggy cocoa-frosted hair, highlighted in spots by the lighter shades of brown, mimicking his Akita coloring. His face, though . . . I looked sheepishly about the room, and to my chagrin, found Matt staring at me.

Ugh. Don't get me wrong: Matt was hotness personified, with his dark complexion, shoulder-length and just-shy-of-black curls, and his pretty boy face. He was the epitome of sex appeal, and he knew it—worked it, even. He was shorter and a little stockier in build than Curjan, but he was all man.

The ladies dug him.

Curjan's dark good looks were more dangerous, deadly. If he'd wanted to play the part of pretty boy he probably could have, but it was evident that he held no interest in making himself attractive or even cared how his looks affected women (or men, as the case may be) around him.

That intrigues me all the more, dognabbit.

Curjan shook his head, much like he would were he still a dog. It couldn't be easy shifting back to human form after 18 years spent as a canine. I wondered what was going on in his head, and the temptation to sneak a mindlink tether in his general direction to do a little snooping was strong. But, I wasn't good enough to not get caught yet, so that was sure to end in an intrusive and extremely awkward way.

I'd have to keep my grubby little mindlink mitts to myself. For now, at least.

The man-dog in question wavered and almost fell, but Dad caught him, just as Bradley flashed back into the room with the water, sodas, and sandwiches. Curjan swiped a water, downing the bottle in a flat three seconds. He then wiped his mouth, grabbed the coke out of Bradley's hands, and did the same with it, ripping out an impressive belch afterward. He grinned and pounded himself on the chest, the rest of the room breaking into laughter as we watched him slowly come back to life.

He then handed Samantha a water, and she gulped hers too, although she did take a little more time to savor the cool liquid as it went down. The calories and caffeine in the soda perked her up, and she looked about the room with more interest, less withdrawn than mere moments before.

I guessed it was true, then, that these guys really could

heal themselves from most anything, given a dose of food and water for their systems to use as fuel. *Fascinating.*

Curjan courteously accepted the offered sandwich from Bradley's outstretched hand but devoured it within seconds, inhaling the bag of chips that came next, too. I remembered how starved Dad had been when we'd rescued him last week, and my heart broke for both of these warriors who'd endured so much on behalf of king and country.

When he'd eaten all available to him (and sent Bradley for more), he was finally ready to use actual sentences, which probably felt weird after all these years.

"King Randulf," he clapped Dad on the shoulder, tears in his eyes. "You have no idea how pleased I am to see you alive and well. What happened? Why are we here? The last I remember we were running through the Appalachian forest as dogs, and suddenly I felt my memories of Perrin slipping away. After that, everything becomes a blur." He kneeled before my father. "I failed you, Your Highness. It was my job to protect you, and I did not succeed in that goal."

The King got teary-eyed himself, pulling Curjan to his feet and embracing him in a manly version of a hug. "Non-sense, my son. It was not you who failed me, but I who failed all my warriors, and for that I am genuinely sorry." He held up his index finger, continuing. "Yet still, before we take on blame for things lying outside our power to control, know that much of the fault lies with Phoebus and his followers. We knew not what we were up against, or that there was an underground army waiting to pounce as soon as feral mind struck me—er, us. More on that later. Of utmost importance now is the following question: do you remember any sort of key you were supposed to be guarding in that salvage yard?"

Curjan looked confused. "Key? Pardon me, Sir, but I was lucky to have enough wits about me to survive each horrific day out there on that chain . . . are you telling me we were put there to guard something? A key?"

Charlie spoke up then, his Brit-influenced accent in full swing. "Would you two kindly allow the king, Baylee, and I access into your minds using our grouplink? Everyone we've rescued so far has been mindswiped or mindblocked, and these tactics have prevented them from remembering or accessing much of their past. If we can remove the blocks from your minds, perhaps you'll remember more and we can gain a clue as to the location of the next key. Baylee and I have formed an especially strong mindmeld that enables us to bring people around and blast through the blockages. When we add in the king we are nigh unstoppable."

Curjan volunteered, nodding his head. "Of course; do mine first while Samantha rests."

Charlie's voice slipped into my head, offering up a warning. "Go easy on this one, Baylee. For whatever reason, you have a super strong connection with him. Remember, we want to remove a blockage, not fry his brain." Dad chuckled.

"Har har," I said, smirking despite myself. "I'll do my best to keep his gray matter intact, just for you. Why don't you two mind your own beeswax, and lend me some of that awesome power so I can get my job done. You ready?"

We linked into Curjan's mind, and immediately ran into a similar blockage to the one we'd found in Dad, Krupert, and Merle. By now Charlie and I were becoming adept at bringing people back to us, but with Dad added into the mix, our powers were astonishing. He used his mindlink-slink to slip through to the other side of the blockage and loosen it, while Charlie and I tethered our minds together to blast through from the front. Between the three of us, we had the mental wall down in minutes, and jumped out just in time to see Curjan slump to the bed, dead asleep.

Huh. That's never happened before.

Ruth felt for a pulse, and it was strong and steady, so we concluded that he just needed a nap as part of his body's efforts to heal.

Next we worked on Samantha's, but her mind proved to be a little different. The blockage was dried out and withered—in fact her entire mind appeared shriveled. When we got inside, Dad was able to easily walk right past the blockage inside her brain, noting that it resembled more a raisin than the plump and hydrated grape it should have been. We were all baffled.

After consulting with Dad and Charlie, I pulled Ruth into the mindlink with us; maybe in her years as a healer she'd seen or dealt with something of this nature before. She explained to us that Samantha had become so depressed, so despondent out on that chain, that she'd given up on life. She's stopped trying to survive—and without access to nourishment, her mind had responded by shriveling, even taking the mindblock with it.

This was going to take more than a simple energy blast, my instinct told me. Ruth suggested that I put my newly-awakened healing energy to use, by sending a wave of green ooze into her mind to heal it first back to a normal mindstate. THEN I could go in with Dad and Charlie to remove the blockage.

We'd try it. With Dad keeping to his location on the other side of the withered barrier, and Charlie and I maintaining our position on the front side of it, I focused on opening my heart and pushing out a wave of love, much as I'd done involuntarily with Mom when I first learned the benefits of my new heart gift.

"Be prepared for a massive burst of waterworks as soon as we're done here," I drawled sardonically to Dad, Charlie, and Ruth. "Everyone the green wave has touched has been overcome with emotion, and I highly doubt poor Samantha will be any different."

Samantha's mind and brain soaked up the healing energy like a sponge, and quickly expanded to fill the space in her head, the barrier engorging as well. When her mind again presented as "normal", we blasted it with our combined tether energy and celebrated as it fell away, hopefully leaving behind the repressed memories for us to work with.

As expected, the second we pulled out of her mind, the sobs began. We were prepared this time, and Ruth cradled her as she cried, great wrenching wails wringing from her vocal cords.

"Where am I, King," she finally asked, looking to Dad for answers, sounding worn yet back in control of her faculties.

"We're on Earth, in New York City, Samantha," he said gently, taking her hand. "Do you remember anything that happened to you, and most importantly, do you have any memories of a key?"

She shook her head, eyes drooping. "Can we talk about this in 15 minutes, Your Highness? I think I might need a short nap."

And with that she was out, too.

Well, that was enlightening. Not.

Chapter 9: Food, Fun, Frolic, and Froth

While Curjan and Samantha took their first naps as humans in over 18 years, the rest of us showered and changed for what could be a long night.

Hunger had struck a crowd that was always looking to eat anyway—with a vengeance—so we took a vote and decided to order pizza so we could watch over the sleeping members of Dad's team while we ate. The credit card would take another hit, but we still needed to hoard our cash for emergencies, so Mom would have to go the quadruple heart attack route when I got home.

One of the local places was offering a vegan pie with all the toppings, so I ordered ten larges with a bunch of sodas and some chips, too. We settled down to wait, some of the team napping, while others conversed quietly. The mood was decidedly somber.

Matt came over and shoved me playfully, giving me his best puppy dog eyes. "I'm sorry I've been such a jealous butt, Baylee," he said, chagrined. "I guess this makes us even for your green-eyed monster showing up at school when I flirted with Amaya and her friends, eh?" He looked at me hopefully.

I skewered him with my haughtiest dirty looks. "I don't think so, my friend. For one thing you actually WERE flirting with them, whereas I was an innocent bystander in the whole 'hey, look, there's your mate' thing. I don't know where we stand, but I was into you, and I was really enjoying getting to know you better. Except now I don't feel like I was special to you at all—just another girl who occupied your wandering eye for a passing moment of time, and who you treated like crappola when things went a little bit haywire."

"Hey, that's not true, cutie," he replied, rubbing my arm. "I'm just as attracted to you as you are to me, which is why I've been behaving so badly. If I didn't care, I wouldn't have any reason to feel jealousy when it comes to you and Curjan. How about we start over . . . as friends, first. Then we'll see if anything builds from there. You're way too young to settle down anyway, plus we have this whole 'end of the world' crisis to get through first. We couldn't afford to get too wrapped up in each other anyway, right?" His big eyes gazed earnestly into mine.

My heart gave a tug. There wasn't a doubt in my mind that I was still attracted to him, and he did have a point that I too had taken a ride on the crazy train when I got jealous. . .

So I skooched over and leaned into him, enjoyed the warmth and clean-smelling maleness he exuded. "Ok, I give, friend." I smiled, glad our weirdness was over and hopeful we could move forward from here.

Why am I suddenly attracted to him again? Reverse psychology! Sneaky bastage.

"So, are you ticklish, Matt?" I questioned innocently, readying myself to attack.

"Ticklish? What's that?" he asked, genuinely confused.

"You don't know what ticklish is?" I grinned, and even I could feel my smile oozing evil. Without uttering another word, I jumped him, digging into both sides of his ribcage, and then moving to above his knees, and finally to his feet. He attempted to defend against the onslaught, but collapsed in a fit of laughter, screaming "Stop, you maniac. What are you doing? It hurts, it hurts!"

Guess everyone's awake now. Oops!

I continued, though, single-minded in my assault, and didn't notice at first when he got his wits about him enough to use the same tactic against me. He lunged and pinned me between his legs, mimicking my moves, and eliciting peals of shrieking laughter from me.

Not bad for his first time.

Suddenly his weight lifted from on top of me, and he was picked up and thrown across the room, hitting the wall and landing in a heap on the far bed. Everyone fell silent, gaping. I rolled to my feet and into ready stance . . . had we been attacked by the Foul Faction?

Only to come face to face with a seething Curjan.

I scrambled back.

Yikes. What in all Holy Hades.

"Whoa, buddy," I backed up, hands in the air. "What gives, what are you doing?"

"Saving you, of course," he replied huffily, as if that was blatantly obvious. "I've known Matt many years, but have never seen him try to harm a teammate before. I understand you're to be our people's savior, but if you can't even defend yourself against one of our own, how do you expect to rescue Perrin?"

I felt my blood begin to boil, and if I could, I'd froth at the mouth, too, just for good measure. "Listen here, Cursive," I poked him in the chest with my finger. "Matt and I were simply PLAYING. It's something people who like each other do here on Earth. Since you appear to have a stick stuck so far up your behind it will never see the light of day, perhaps you aren't familiar with this practice. What we were doing was called 'tickling'. Have you never heard of it?" I moved toward him, intent on providing him a little show and tell.

He backed up then, face turning red, holding out his hands to ward me off. "Listen, Child, I get that you have a lot to learn about me and my job as your father's second in command, but I don't PLAY, and certainly not with those who might technically be considered my bosses. I don't know what this 'tickling' is, but it appeared to me that Matt was injuring you, and you were screaming. So I intervened. It won't happen again." He stiffly and huffily turned back to the bed where Matt was picking himself up.

Curjan reached out a hand in olive branch to help Matt off the bed, but Matt pushed it aside, saying, "Just stay out of my way, Curjan. While I'm glad you're alive and out of that horrible situation, I have no need to be your best bud. Don't touch me again unless you mean business. Got it?"

"Got it." Curjan smirked, pacing away.

There was just a little too much testosterone in the room for my taste. I flounced out the door and down the hall to the elevators, so irritated that I'd be just as glad not to see either of those two men for the next twenty years. Or longer.

Dad popped into my head. "Baylee, honey, don't go too far. While I don't suspect that the Double N's will find us all the way across the city, I don't want anyone going off alone, especially you, not right now. Are you ok?"

I sighed, shoulders slumping. I really needed a moment of solitude to clear my head. Both Mom and I were used to lots of alone time, with the exception of our animal companions, and all these people being up my beehive 24/7 was really starting to get to me.

Pouting, I turned and dragged myself back to the room, where an incredibly awkward silence ensued. Returning the favor to Dad, I popped into his head. "There, you happy now? This paradise is your fault for making me come back; you should have just let me have a moment or two to get myself together."

"Oh, honey," he said. "It will all work itself out. We needed to have a meeting anyway, to see if Curjan and Samantha remember anything more and plan what comes next."

"Fine," I plopped down onto the floor. "Let's get this over with."

Just then there was a knock on the door.

Saved by the pizza.

CHAPTER 10: DOWN TO BEESWAX

Bellies full, we settled down to discuss what happened today and brainstorm where the next key could be hidden. Dad caught Curjan and Samantha up on all that had happened in the past week, and then we sat back to hear what they remembered.

Samantha was glowing by now, having been treated with the ooze of green, eaten twice, showered, and gotten ahold of some clean clothes. Hope poured from every pore of her body, and she kept glancing at Curjan with grateful eyes. Twinges of jealousy tugged at my innards again, but I blithefully ignored them. *Go away, stupid unwanted-and-unasked-for feelings.*

She spoke softly. "I want to thank Curjan first and foremost for keeping me alive all these years when I just wanted to die. Even though I couldn't remember much about my life, I knew that I had a family somewhere and I missed them so dreadfully that I couldn't go on. He refused to give up, and prodded me unmercifully at times to hold onto life. As I now realize, we weren't really capable of dying from starvation and thirst, but we sure did suffer for it." A tear tracked its way down her cheek.

"Now that I look back on it with fresh eyes, I can see that

they wanted us in perpetual hunger and pain so that we'd be meaner if anyone did come searching for whatever it was we were placed there to guard. Curjan killed many ninjas, as you call them. I'm not sure if they were sent as tests, or if he actually got to some of their guard. But regardless, he reduced their numbers by around 50 men and women over the last 18 years that we languished in that junkyard."

Curjan crossed the room to her, draping his arm across her shoulders. It was a caring gesture from a man who seemed uncomfortable with showing emotion, and I watched him closely, curious to learn more about what made him tick.

Samantha turned toward the king. "Sir, now that I have memories of my past life, all I want, all I can think of, is returning to my husband and my twins, who would be adults themselves by now, just a couple years older than Baylee. I've missed so much of their lives . . . I don't even know what remains to go back to, but I know I can't focus until I see for myself. May I please be released from my tenure in your guard, at least for a few months, to pick up the pieces of my family life and hopefully glue it back together?"

Dad looked grim, but quickly acquiesced. "Of course, Samantha, it's the least I can do given all the pain I've caused you and your family. What we thought would be a two-year mission turned out to be more like twenty years. As soon as we get back to Culpeper, we'll arrange for you to return home and bring a replacement member from Perrin for my team. But first, can you tell us if you remember anything at all helpful from your life chained in the salvage yard?"

She shook her head. "Honestly, not at the moment. It sounds like you endured the same kind of torture we did. Hunger, thirst, ninjas dressed in black abusing you. I never had an inkling we were there to guard anything, and now that most of my earlier memories are intact, the ones from all these years of torture are fading into a blur. If I remember anything, anything at all, I'll let you know immediately."

I broke in. "I didn't yet hear what happened when we grabbed Curjan and Samantha and flashed. How did Rebecca and Matt get injured?"

Rebecca spoke up. "I was on the front line, and didn't see the guy flash behind me. He hit me on the back of the head, and as I was falling the guy in front of me lashed out, too. Luckily, our team had my back, and Ruth and Daniel stood over me while fighting off the ninjas until you were safely free and we could flash away. Then they grabbed me up, and the rest you know."

Matt looked sheepish. "There was this huge guy on Team Ugly, and he stomped really hard on my foot, which I wasn't expecting. I mean, who does that? I think he broke a couple of bones, because it was agonizing, but I'm all healed up now, see?" He held up his foot, twirling it around as if to impress the ladies, aka, me. He vaunted his eyebrows at me, wagging them in a flirtatious manner, and I couldn't hold back a guffaw. *OK, he's adorkable when he's playful.*

"So," I looked at Curjan, reluctantly. I knew I'd have to get over our earlier squabble, since we had to work together, but it wasn't easy. "Why were you and Samantha free, anyway? How did that happen?"

"Well," he explained. "We were desperate, and out of that desperation we attempted a plan we'd been able to patch together. Since we were feral, we couldn't really talk to each other, but we could communicate via basic images. I got an idea of trussing a ninja up with both our chains, so we tried it. It worked better than we could have imagined, because the chain acted as a mind tether, and the guy became part of our pack, in essence. We overtook his mind, forced him to release us, then did what we had to do." His expression turned sour as he remembered the killings.

"Then the sirens went off, we ran for our lives, and that's when we intersected with you all. I'm not one to be overly-emotional, but you have our eternal gratitude, because we surely would have been caught without your intervention. Thank you, everyone." He swept his glance around the room to include all of us.

"It was nothing," I blushed, like I did it all myself. *Oh, brother. What is wrong with me?*

Charlie shot me an amused glance. "Did you know that young Baylee here had a vision of where you were, and hounded us until we came to get you?"

Curjan looked confused. "Oh, really?"

Jake couldn't help himself; turns out he was the blabbermouth of the bunch, and he blurted out the truth I'd do anything to hide. . . . And I was gonna string him up by his you-know-whats for it too. "Yeah, she says you're her mate."

The room fell silent, you could have heard the proverbial pin drop. *Oh, bloody Hades.*

Curjan looked stricken, whatever modicum of color he'd managed to get back into his face fell away, and he sat heavily onto the bed. I was mortified.

As much as I wanted to slink away and hide, something took over, and I went in the opposite direction. *Go figure.*

I stepped to the front of the group and pulled myself up, turning to address everyone. "Ok, well, the secret's out there then, thanks for that, Jake. I owe you one." He had the grace to appear chagrined, at least. I continued. "We obviously have more important things to be worrying about. I no more want a mate than Curjan here does, so let's talk about the Foul Faction of Nefarious Ninjas and not my non-existent love life, thank you very much."

I flounced to the nearest chair and plopped down in it like I hadn't a care in the world. I don't know where that came from, but it felt good not to be the cowardly little wab-bit sometimes. *Screw 'em all.* Truth be told, it made me wish I was still a little girl, so I didn't even need to THINK about men and how annoying they could be.

I suddenly missed Amaya so, so much. All this adulting meant I'd lost my friendship with one of the most important people in my life. I had been forced to keep her out of the loop, and we'd never kept secrets from each other before. EVER. So here I was, lying nonstop, avoiding her, telling her without words that she wasn't important to me, when all that couldn't be further from the truth.

I needed to be with her, to tell her everything—about Matt and Curjan, yes—but also about The Scion, and the end of the world as we knew it.

These were life-changing moments, and here I was with-out a best friend to bounce it all off of. *Ugh.*

I got out my phone to see if Amaya had responded to any of my last 3,579 texts, but alas, no go. She was really mad, and I didn't know how I was gonna fix it.

I sighed, pushing all that to the back of my brain stem. I had to get my mind back in the game—this terrifying, hor-rible life and death game I'd suddenly found myself a major player in.

I realized Dad was talking, and I should actually be pay-ing attention. I tuned into the conversation in time to hear him say "I don't see any way around it. We need to sneak back into that complex disguised as a junkyard and see what we can find. Thoughts?"

I looked at the clock. Midnight. *Talk about a whole day getting away from you!* I realized it was probably better to go in under cover of darkness, but it certainly held little appeal to my scaredy-cat nature.

There were murmurings of agreement or dissent, but by now I could barely hold my eyes open.

"Um, Dad, do you think we could take a little nap first? I mean, I know that Curjan and Samantha just woke up, but the rest of us have been going nonstop all day. I can't believe it was just 15 hours ago I woke up in Culpeper. I really need to catch a catnap before we go, and I'd imagine most of the others would agree."

Nods followed.

Charlie loved his catnaps, and I smiled as I remember the first day I met him, in his gray kitty form, and how he'd curled up on my bed and I snuggled with him. I guess those days were over . . . now that I knew as a human he looked like a middle-aged (but still handsome) uncle, there would be no more snuggles.

Way too creepified.

Dad reluctantly assented to the nap idea. "Fine, everyone, one hour cat or dog nap, depending on your preference, and then we're going in. Curjan and Samantha, are you able to join us? You may have a better idea where to search since you spent so much time there, or your memory could be jogged by something."

Samantha immediately began shaking and reverting to

her shell-shocked persona, crawling toward Curjan and huddling against him. Yeah, there was that ever-present twinge of jealousy, but more than that I felt an overwhelming sense of compassion for her. She had not held up well to the torture, and I couldn't blame her for never wanting to step foot in that place again.

Unbidden, the green wave emanated from my heart, engulfing both Samantha and Curjan in it's healing energy. Samantha's shoulders wracked with fresh sobs, and even the stoic Curjan got a little verklempt, wiping at his eyes and turning his face toward the wall. Both she and Curjan agreed a little more sleep might be in order for them, too.

Folks grabbed a spot on the floor, bed, or chair in the two-room suite, and as long as everyone was willing to get cozy, we had enough sleeping space for everyone. I sidled my way over and onto the bed with Tara, believing it safer all the way around to snooze beside her instead of any beings of the male persuasion.

She nodded in welcome, and we both settled down to catch a few zzzz's.

Before I knew it, it was 1:45 a.m., and I was being jogged awake by Dad and Charlie. We were slated to flash to Big A Auto Salvage at 2:00 a.m., and although all I wanted to do was sleep, I reasoned that if all went well we could flash back here and slip in a few more winks later.

I jumped into the mental meetup with Dad, Charlie, Daniel, and Curjan, and it was decided that Samantha should definitely stay behind. The odds of her falling apart out there were good, and we really needed to be on our toes. Starting out with a certain liability wasn't the way to play it.

Tara, our resident scientist turned doctor turned chef

decided to stay behind with her, as did Rebecca and Matt. Both had healed well from their earlier physical confrontations, but nine of us would be plenty to handle a search of the salvage property, and there was safety in numbers.

I knew that Curjan was Dad's second in command, as Daniel was Charlie's, but I was immediately impressed with his diligence and air of authority. He seemed pretty much back to normal, despite the horrific circumstances he'd endured until just a few hours ago. He'd gotten right back into the saddle—or whatever the dog analogy might be—and he seemed beyond thrilled to know he was part of something that mattered, something beyond the life of a chained junkyard dog.

Curjan was determined to earn his keep and work his hardest to ensure we won this war. I couldn't ask more than that of anybody.

CHAPTER 11: AUTO SALVAGE, OR AUTO SAVAGE?

We readied ourselves, and then flashed in two squads inside the perimeter of the junkyard to the spot we'd hid out earlier—just before the blind turn behind the pile of squished cars.

I would have said it was déjà vu, except that this time it was dark and eerily quiet. No one made a peep as we assessed the danger, or lack thereof. When we sensed no one was there, we slipped around the corner and stalked down the dirt path toward the area where Curjan and Samantha had been imprisoned. Curjan put his nose to the air, sniffing, and I smirked at the fact that he still acted like a dog much of the time. I assumed after spending 18 years as his Akita counterpart, he wouldn't even realize he did it, which made it PDC—pretty darn cute.

His hair fell across his face, and he pushed it back in irritation. He lifted his nose again, scenting the breeze. He narrowed his eyes and pointed in the direction of his former "home." We followed him, everyone alert for threats. He linked up with us through our mental tethers, and his voice came into my head.

"The smell of this place is giving me some flashbacks, Sir; I hope I can hold it together." He looked at my father. "I say we explore that area first, because it stands to reason if we were guarding something, it would have been there. But, if I lose it, I will need someone to make sure I don't endanger the mission. Take me out if you must."

"The same thing happened to me in the spot where I'd been chained, Son, so you aren't alone in this. Baylee, you and Charlie stay close to Curjan. If he needs support, link up and jump into his mind to keep him from going feral again. The rest of you, spread out. Look for any clues as to where the key might be. Bring anything unusual to the attention of Daniel or myself. Here we go."

Curjan stepped around the corner, through an open doorway, and into the cleared space between salvage areas. It looked like an arena in a dystopian novel, with walls and mounds of junked vehicles and other metal scraps piled high to create a perimeter. There were two rundown dog-houses, much like my father's, both incapable of providing shelter from the elements for any dog.

I was overwhelmed with disgust. The area had never been cleaned, and I was hit with the smell of feces and urine that coated the ground. Both Dad and Curjan seemed on the verge of being triggered by the memories invoked through the scent and sight of the appalling living conditions.

Reminding myself that I had to let go of my own outrage in order to help them, I tried to distract them with talk of the key. "What if they did the exact same thing with his key that they did with yours, Dad? What if his stake opens up another underground bunker? Which reminds me . . . we're probably on camera right now."

I looked around, picturing the area as I'd seen it on the screen from the bunker by my house. I turned in the direction the camera should be, scouring the garbage for any obvious signs of it. With so much metal and junk piled up, the task would not be an easy one. Besides, if they were watching us via the camera feed, it was too late anyway—they knew we were here.

Curjan rushed over and yanked his stake from the ground, but nothing happened. Samantha's stake yielded no results either. Everyone flashed to the perimeter of the arena and began to search, although we had no way of knowing exactly what we were searching for.

I finally found the camera, ripping it from its hiding spot. Beneath it rested a square of white paper, so I grabbed that too, shoving it into my pocket to read when I had more light. I decided to take the camera with me, plopping it into my backpack; maybe the tech team could do something with it.

Bradley and Smith chimed into the group mindlink. "Here, everyone, we found something." I flashed myself across the arena to see them digging a metal box out of the ground. It had been at the very edge of the junk pile, and just within reach of Curjan's chain, which would make sense from a protection standpoint. They'd want to make sure anyone who came looking for it had to get through the angry and starving Akita before reaching their prize.

Smith made short work of the latch, snipping it off, the metal sheared clean in half. He eagerly whipped open the box lid, triggering a loud and raucous alarm. *Uh oh.* A piece of paper lay where the key presumably had been, and all it said was "Looking for something, ladies and gents? Back to the drawing board."

Frustrated, Smith threw the box across the lot, and the alarm emanating from it slowed to a jagged whine and then stopped. We were all aware that between the camera and the alarm we'd tripped, we either had to get out of there ASAP, or prepare to stand and fight.

Just as we'd decided to flash ourselves back to the hotel suite to regroup, a solitary ninja appeared at the entrance of the arena.

The guy was shorter than Dad's 6'4" and Curjan's 6'2", but not by much. He probably went about 6', and—like all these guys—looked like he spent way too much time at the gym. I was exhausted just thinking about it. His head was covered by the ninja mask, and what was visible of his face was indistinguishable from the dark shadows of night.

He stood unmoving in the doorway, as if he could see us better than we could him and was memorizing our faces. I didn't like it. I felt uneasy in his presence, and I could sense that the others did as well. If this move was done to intimidate us, it was working. We assumed ready stances, yet he still didn't move to attack or retreat.

Finally, he spoke. "I have a message for The Beguiler, from King Phoebus and The Scion. Turn yourself in to us now, today, and save your family and your little animal friends. We know of the prophecy, and we will not tolerate your interference with our plans for this planet." He looked directly at me as he spoke (so much for incognito), and I shifted nervously. He held out his hand to me. "Come with me, please."

I laughed. "The Beguiler? Ha, I wish! Are you a freaking lunatic, man? I'll go with you the day Hades ices over. And if you think you're going to threaten my family and myself and have me simply roll over, then you've got another think comin'. Back off, Bucko."

I flashed to his side and slammed my fist into his face before he even knew what hit him. He quickly recovered and lashed out, grabbing my wrist and attempting to take me to wherever evil ninjas take their prey. *Maybe I shoulda' thought that through.*

Thank Dogness, though, he was unsuccessful; for in that instant Curjan, who'd shifted to Akita form, appeared, grabbed the man by the neck, and unceremoniously ripped his throat from his body. The man's face still wore a look of shock as the last gurgle of lifeblood seeped into the already-desecrated ground.

Well, that's one way to do it, I thought dazedly, before I promptly bent over and heaved up the remains of the pizza I'd had earlier.

I then sank to the ground, trying to avoid sitting in the man's blood and my own vomit. *What in the ever-lovin' netherworld,* I mumbled to myself before shock turned my brains and limbs to jelly.

Chapter 12: Murder, Mayhem, Mystery, and Memorabilia

Chaos ensued, and I was barely aware of being picked up by Smith and thrown over his shoulder, then flashing immediately to the hotel. He put me down on the bed where I'd napped earlier, and I lulled to the side, catching myself with my elbow, my mind in a fog. Tara and Ruth rushed over, checking me for injuries.

I was embarrassed that there wasn't anything wrong with me other than simple squeamishness, so I motioned them away. Admittedly, I hadn't handled that development well, but—coming out of nowhere—I was mentally unprepared for my first upclose look at death. *And a grisly one at that.*

At the reminder, I rushed for the bathroom—shoving through anyone standing in my way—and heaved up the remnants of the remnants that hadn't been previously heaved. I brushed my teeth and looked at myself in the mirror. My green eyes were cloudy with shock and anguish, and my normally-pale face appeared even whiter than usual. I'd thrown my auburny-brown locks up in a semi-neat ponytail earlier, but it was now disheveled and pieces of hair had escaped and were flailing about.

I felt like I was covered in the ninja's blood, even though I saw not a speck on me. I ditched my clothes anyway and took a long, hot shower, scrubbing my skin until it felt raw. I still sported an invisible film of dirt and guilt, but I knew I couldn't hide in the bathroom forever. I dried off, let my hair hang about my shoulders, and dug the remaining outfit from my backpack.

I then made my way out of the bathroom, avoiding eye contact with…everyone. My feelings were a jumbled mess. I knew this was war, I knew there was no way around death and killing, but I also felt that Curjan went overboard by ripping that guy apart in front of me like that, when we could have arrested him and transported him back to Perrin for questioning.

I mean, if we didn't have arrest powers—with the King, his deputy, and Charlie as one of his top ranking officials, then who did?

Logically, I understood that Dad, Curjan, and Samantha were all suffering their own forms of PTSD from years of imprisonment and brutality. Dad had transformed into his shepherd counterpart and slain a ninja himself mere days ago, so I got that they might go berserk and go for the jugular when confronted with one of their torturers.

It just seemed to me that we needed to be better than them. If they've been mutilating and killing our people all these years, but we off them too instead of arresting and questioning them, then aren't we the same? I knew it wasn't cut and dry, black and white, but I wanted us to start with some kind of rules of engagement.

Everyone got quiet when I walked into the living room, and—having made up my mind—I turned to face them all.

"This was my first time seeing death up close and personal, and I feel responsible for that man's demise because I got cocky and attacked him. This forced Curjan into taking action to protect me as the king's daughter, so in the end what happened is on me.

"Thank you for saving my life, Curjan, and I don't want to seem ungrateful. I'd just like to discuss some ground rules for us when dealing with these ninjas. I believe we should be arresting them and sending them to Perrin to be questioned by what I presume are experts in the field, rather than simply slaying them. Not only are we losing critical avenues of information, but some of them could be mindwiped or controlled in some other way by Phoebus and his minions. They may not be inherently evil people, but we won't know that unless we give them a chance to be restored to the person they were in the past."

I took a deep breath, grabbed myself by the courage, and continued. "I understand by doing so we're taking a chance of them spying from within, but my gut tells me they've already infiltrated our ranks. So shouldn't we be imprisoning them and gathering intelligence from them, too? Thoughts?"

Dad smiled at me, nodding his head, then popped into my mind with a quick, affirmative "So proud of you, honey."

He turned to the team, saying "Baylee has a point. I have behaved no better than Curjan, as you're well aware. I was, and still am, filled with rage at what these men and women did to me and my people for the past 18 years. When I saw the man who'd tortured me, I immediately and without thought transformed and killed him—and I won't say I regret it. Curjan has suffered the same abusive conditions, and we put him into a setting that was anything but condu-cive to his healing. As such, it would be naïve to expect him to react any differently than I did." He looked around the room.

"I agree with a general policy of capture instead of kill. However, I will clarify that with a caveat: if it comes down to your death or the death of a Nefarious Ninja," he smirked at me "then it's an obvious choice. I don't totally agree with Baylee that this man's life should have been spared. He threatened not only her life but the lives of my soon-to-be-wife and our animal companions. Even if he were just the messenger, I don't blame Curjan for making the choice he did. That man could have flashed away with Baylee and we wouldn't have known where to find her. I, for one, am very grateful to you, Curjan, for saving my daughter's life." He bowed in Cur's direction.

Curjan nodded regally to The King, then briefly looked my way, saying, "You're welcome, Princess," and turned aside.

Well, alrighty then. Butthead.

Fireworks over, at least for now, our resident tech expert, Curtis, and Jake, Matt's twin and Curtis' sidekick, pored over the camera to see if anything could be gleaned from it. The rest of us mulled over what we found—or didn't find—on site, and where we went from here.

When the camera turned up nothing of use, we were admittedly at a dead end, out of ideas. I remembered that I left my credit card in my old (and, to my mind, blood-cov-ered) jeans, so I dug into my backpack to grab it out before I lost it. As I searched the pockets, the white slip of paper that had been stashed beneath the camera fell out and onto the floor. When I bent down to pick it up, I saw only three words on it.

MOMA. WATCH VIDEO.

That was it.

Huh? Is someone trying to help us?

I ran over to Dad and Charlie, shoving the note in their faces in my excitement. "Look what I found under the camera when I yanked it out! What does this mean?"

Dad and I looked at each other in a panic. "They're going after Mom, aren't they?" I cried. "We have to leave, NOW, Dad. NOW!!!"

I raced around the room throwing stuff into my backpack like a crazy person. Everyone else looked to Dad for guidance, and seeing that he was pretty much doing the same thing, decided we must be heading home after all.

Dad threw a long-distance mindlink to Rupert to check on Mom and let him know we were on our way back. Rupert affirmed that all had been quiet there, with the exception of an angry Momma Bear, of course. Given the warning tone of the note, he agreed it wouldn't be a bad idea to regroup at home and go from there.

Feeling defeated, and in no way in possession of anything resembling the second key, we began to retrace our steps— first flashing in groups to the Philly train station, and then hopping another train to Baltimore, where we could flash directly to our house in Culpeper.

I was looking forward to curling up, even for a little while, with my BooBoo, Una, Tootie, and my favorite pup Khronos. I avoided sitting with anyone on the train trip home so I didn't have to make small talk or pretend I was ok, thereby freeing myself up to pout and fret at will. I didn't waste any time getting down to business, worrying about Mom and whether the ninjas were indeed plotting to take away my family and my pets.

I could live without many things, but I knew deep in my gut that those were the things I could not live without.

Now the fight was becoming personal. I was going to be forced to come out swinging, and I was well aware that I'd need a teensy bit more training if I were gonna take down ninjas in order to protect my family.

I looked in Curjan's direction, where he napped in the seat next to Dad. Despite my weird fascination with the guy, and the fact that we already rubbed each other the wrong way, something told me he'd be the man to train me. Which meant I'd have to suck up my pride and ask him for help if I wanted to be the best.

And I needed to be the best; my family's safety was at stake.

Sigh. Just my luck.

Chapter 13: Momma Bear

We walked in the door to screaming and the sound of smashing glass. *What in the herd of antelopes is going on here?*

It turned out the Mominator was coming in hot, and Dad had had the misfortune to be in the first group to arrive home. *Yikes.* I felt for him. Mom was in no way abusive, never had been, but once in awhile something would make her toss her calm cookies, and there would be drama and screeching and whatever-was-nearby-throwing.

I guessed she was in the kitchen, and our drinkware was not faring well as a result.

I rushed inside, not because I was eager to join the mayhem, but because maybe—once she saw her one and only not-quite-adult daughter was still in one piece—just maybe, she would calm down.

Things didn't go as planned. When she saw me, her expression turned murderous as opposed to the beatific I'd hoped for. *Uh oh.* She began advancing toward me, and in my panic, the green heart chakra ooze spewed out and enveloped her. Dad gave me the look, but I simply shrugged my shoulders.

Truth be told, I wasn't exactly yet in control of my

"love smog"; it had a mind of its own. It seemed when I was around my family—and was feeling stressed or lovey dovey—that crap just eeked on out like it owned the place.

Dad caught Mom as she swooned, a new reaction to my love drug. It was probably the mashup of her extreme angst—if we could call her maniacal breakdown a simple case of nerves—and my dose of "open heart, insert love" slamming into each other and causing her brain to malfunction. *Ha!*

I wasn't concerned that she'd been harmed in any way, but Tara checked her out just in case. While she was out, we took our few moments of reprieve to fill Krupert and Merle in on what had gone down in NYC.

Mom's bestie Janie had gone home after awakening from her earlier dose of mindbind, mumbling about not being able to miss any more work due to this insanity, but other than that Krupert said they'd noticed nothing amiss. No one had tried to enter, and everyone in the house was safe.

We need to move. I knew it, my gut knew it, and now I needed to convince everyone else, including Mom, which wouldn't be easy.

I cleared my throat. "So, it appears, for the moment anyway, Mom is safe, albeit a little off her rocker. But I have to believe that note was a warning from someone who is on our side in all this. Who else thinks it's super weird that Dad was chained just down the street from us all these years? Like they were taunting us. They had to have known we were here; and even if they didn't then, and that was all some kind of bizarre coincidence—which I don't believe—they certainly know we're here by now."

I was warming up to my topic. "We have to get out of

here until this war is finished. It's not safe; I know it in my gut. Now that I refused to go with them, they've flat out threatened my mother and our beloved pets. We can't go off and leave them unguarded, and we can't keep enough guards here to stop an invasion AND go in search of the remaining keys and Dad's warriors. We have to find someplace to hole up where they won't find us, or at least is more defensible so they can't get to those who are innocent in all this. Any ideas?"

I stopped for breath. Most of the team was nodding in agreement, and some were murmuring with their neighbors, tossing ideas around.

"It shouldn't be any place where my team stayed while in human form, as I suspect now that we were being watched even then. We could go back to Perrin, and be protected there at the palace and government headquarters, but I'd prefer to stay here so we can search for the keys and my squad. Charlie, is there any place your team found that would be suitable? I highly doubt they were following you, especially since you spent most of your time on Earth as your cat counterparts," Dad said, rubbing his chin in thought.

Bradley, our resident foodie (and munitions specialist—*he cooks bombs AND dinner, boom!*) normally didn't say much, but this time he was the first to chime in. At around 5'10", he was one of the shorter men in the group, and I realized that between his height and his subdued nature, he was too-often overlooked.

I studied him. Bradley was certainly manly and attractive, with a light brown buzz cut, gray-blue eyes, and a no-nonsense attitude. He was quietly sturdy, reliable, with just a hint of the bad boy lurking under the surface. I'd bet chicks dug him once they got around to noticin' him.

"There was this place we spotted when we were investigating the area a couple days ago. We'd caught the scent of a big cat—which were supposedly extinct—and were intrigued. We followed her along a river, but eventually lost the scent. We never did find that elusive bugger, but in our search for her we came across an interesting property. It was about 25 minutes north of here, on the Hazel River, and the home looked big enough to accommodate our needs. More importantly, it sat empty. The house is almost a mile into the woods, and well-insulated from prying eyes. I wonder if we could rent it?"

That being our best (and only) idea, we all voted "yep" to pursuing it further, and Bradley, Charlie, and Smith flashed there again to check it out. It was in excellent condition, and looked like it could readily suit our short-term needs. Curtis found the owner information online and placed a call to the management company. A short five hours later, using a fake name and cash Dad had pulled from a second bank account, Curtis—and by extension the rest of us—were the proud 6-month-leasees of a 60-acre property overlooking a meandering river in the heart of central Virginia.

The only downside to the place, I would quickly learn, was that there was no fencing, no doggie door, and no separate kitty areas. I wasn't leaving without my companion critters, so we'd have to make some quick adjustments within the next few hours to ensure their safety. Luckily, we had the manpower, we just needed someone to head up the project . . . and I knew just the person . . .

When the Mominator woke up she was still a little Grumpypants, but she'd gotten over the worst of it. I hugged her, giving her a smooch on the cheek for good measure. "I love you, Mommy. I'm sorry we went without you . . . but we couldn't risk you OR the team that way. And look, we're back already, so no harm done, right?" I had no plans to tell her about my almost-abduction, and I didn't know if Dad was gonna be that stupid or not, but that would have to be on him.

We needed to tell her something, though, to make her believe we were in enough danger to justify the move. I thought the note would be enough to do the trick, so I pulled it from my pocket. "Mom, Dad told you we need to hide out, right? Did he explain to you about this note we got that seems to be threatening you? We can't protect everyone here, we're just not set up for it, and it's too public. We're vulnerable to attack. We have two choices right now—hunker down or fight—and until we know more of what we're up against and get those keys in our possession, we really can't afford an all-out war. Protecting you and our animals is my number one priority at the moment. So will you please go? I'll be there, too."

Rolling her eyes, she reached for the note, then snorted, dismissively. "MOMA? WATCH VIDEO? What video?" She eyed me, thinking. "Are you sure they weren't meaning MOMA, as in Museum of Modern Art in New York City?"

Oh. What? I was thrown for a loop. No. No, I wasn't sure, at all.

Dad stopped mid-stride. "What? There's a place called MOMA in New York City?"

Mom was a graphic designer, and art was kinda "her

thang." If anyone around here knew about a famous art museum, it would be her. "Yes, we studied it in college, and I've always wanted to go, but didn't want to make the trip to New York. I mean, maybe this person doesn't spell well and was talking about me, but there's a chance they were talking about the museum, too, right? And what video?"

"We haven't figured that part out yet," I said, thinking harder now. "We can't rule out that the person was pointing toward the museum and not you, but my gut is telling me we aren't safe here. And my gut instinct is not like it used to be, Mom. Now it's right, virtually every time, and it's demanding. When it talks to me, we really need to listen. So, between these two things, will you please pack up what you can't live without, and let's go?"

She reluctantly agreed. "I guess I'll work virtually for the time being, instead of doing sitdowns with my clients. Luckily, with today's internet, I can work from anywhere . . . wait, you're not going to stop me from doing that, too, are you?"

Curtis chimed in. "Just stay off the internet as much as you can, and I'll try to get some extra protections in place ASAP. The less we're online, the harder it will be for them to track us and find out where we're staying. We should be safe for a little while at least."

"The place is furnished," Charlie offered up. "So we don't have to take more than the basic necessities. There are four bedrooms upstairs and two below. I know that you'll need one for a temporary cat room, which leaves five bedrooms for the rest of us and the pups. Take blankets, sleeping bags and pillows, and we'll split up and make do on a temporary basis. Everyone, pack your own things, we'll flash as a group, then come back for the animals and other essentials. Questions?"

Despite the unease, an air of excitement took hold—the thrill of the unknown. I'll admit, the idea of living along a river, for even a short while, was like a dream come true for Mom and me. Ironically, it would be under dire circumstances that we achieved said dream, but I intended to take at least one moment to pretend this was my sanctuary in the woods after all. *And I'm a princess living in a palace, too,* I smirked.

Hey, wait a second, I thought . . . . *If I survive this, and Dad remains king, then I guess I would be kinda a princess, wouldn't I? Huh. Imagine that. Why is it, though, that when we girls dream of princessing, it's all sunshine and unicorns— not killing and the fate of the world resting on our shoulders?*

Argh. I can't even do princessing right.

I mentally slapped myself silly. I couldn't afford to live in that world of negative self-talk and pity. I knew we were dead meat if I did. I had to find a way to get and stay positive, and believe in myself and this team, or the destruction of two worlds would be on my head. And that I couldn't stomach.

I reluctantly went in search of Curjan to ask him if he'd train me to fight, but instead ran into Samantha, who was just coming from a talk with Dad—her eyes shining with happiness and tears. I put my hand on her arm. "Are you ok?"

She nodded. "More than ok, actually. I was just able to mindlink with my husband in Perrin, via the help of your father. He has still believed in me, and waited for me, all these years! Can you imagine? He said he never thought I was dead, and he would wait for me for as long as it took for me to come home. I don't know what I've done to deserve such a loving partner, but I'm so incredibly grateful and eager to get home to him and our twins."

I noticed she hadn't mentioned the twins. "Are they girls or boys? Are they alright too?"

Her face darkened. "They're girls, actually. They're about two years older than you are, and they've both been training to be part of the elite guard since they were 15. My husband said they wanted to follow in my footsteps, and were convinced they could come to Earth and find me when they get good enough to make the squad. However, one of them, Lexi, disappeared about six months ago, and hasn't been heard from since. She's opened up communication with my husband only twice in that timeframe, and immediately shut it back down, like she's letting him know she's still alive, but refuses to talk. He's trying to trust that she's on top of whatever it is she's become part of, but we don't know for sure. I need to get home so I can find her."

I frowned, squeezing her shoulder. "I'm so sorry. Hopefully she's fine, and will come home as soon as she knows you're back. She's probably just out exploring or looking for you. When do you leave?"

"As soon as we get set up at the new property, your father told me we'd arrange for a transport tether to get me to Perrin while some more of the elite guard takes my place here. Within a matter of hours, I'll get to see my family again, after 18 years. I can't even imagine it!" She beamed a smile at me, and wandered off, lost in her own little dreamworld.

I couldn't help but feel a momentary surge of jealousy—she gets to leave this burgeoning war and take time off to be with her family. That was a luxury that I didn't have, and while I knew she'd still have the stress of finding her daughter, at least she could rest in the arms of her family for a few days while she gathered her strength.

I forgot about Curjan and training for the time being, and focused on getting my kitties set up in the temporary—and much less awesome—cat room. When I flashed to the new property with Mom and Dad for the first time, my jaw dropped at the vision before me. If Mom and I had been able to purchase our dream property, this would so be it! A stained wooden deck ran from one end of the house to the other, wrapping around the far corner and forming a barbecue and picnic area along the right side. It was like living in a massive treehouse with a panoramic view of the Hazel River, and I pictured us kayaking and swimming in that river with the pups and our own pack of river otters.

Surely there'll be river otters, right?

Cathedral ceilings in the living room opened to large windows and sliding glass doors in the living room and kitchen. Both rooms came complete with skylights, there were stone fireplaces top and bottom floors, and the eat-in kitchen was large enough to accommodate even a crew the size of ours.

The only downside was that, since the house sat atop a hill which sloped to the river, there was no easy way to create a fenced area for the mutts. And they NEEDED a fenced yard. We couldn't allow them to take over the countryside, running amok and slaying all the precious woodland critters. Nope. Couldn't happen.

So I roped in Smith, Matt, and Daniel—the most handy-manny-types of the bunch—and asked them to help me figure out how to quickly throw up a fence for the dogs. We decided to install a doggie door in the basement at the back of the house, and gathered rolls of 6-foot welded wire fencing and posts, with all the necessary tools and accessories, and got to work.

Within hours we had cobbled together a serviceable 1-acre fenced area for the dogs to explore and do their business.

Thank Dog for super-strength and super-speed. And lots of warm bodies.

Now, I just had to hope that the dogs wouldn't try to escape our less-than-secure perimeter . . . because that probably wouldn't end well, for any of us.

Chapter 14: Hiding and Hunkering

Once we'd moved into our temporary safe zone, aka hiding place, and the dogs had a fenced area and place to run and a million new things to sniff, I could finally let my guard down a bit. By now it was nightfall, and I had to step back and take a minute to even get my days straight. I realized I'd only "met" Charlie and his gang last Friday *(did all this really happen in less than a week?)* and we'd only rescued Dad, Krupert, and Merle that weekend. Monday night we'd discovered the first key, and I was knocked unconscious by my exploding heart chakra, and then Tuesday we raced off to New York in search of Curjan and Samantha.

Tuesday night we'd slain a ninja *(ugh, don't remind me)*, and by today, Wednesday morning, we were racing back home to Culpeper to move Mom and our companions to safety. Now here we were, set up in a hideout I'd love to call home, and tomorrow we would presumably plot how to slay our next dragon.

For tonight, I would rest, celebrate our relative security and the rescue of wonderful people I'd never known existed a week ago, and go to sleep surrounded by my animal loves.

Tomorrow I'd deal with the fact that I'd missed two days of school, and worry about how to get back into my bestie's good graces. We were done with school now until after New Years, Thank Dog—since Sunday was Christmas—and within that time frame we could theoretically get our hands on the second key and figure out where to look for the third.

If I wanted to graduate with a decent-enough GPA to be accepted into college (which, granted, seemed a little pointless right now), I couldn't afford to miss more school. Yet compared to the fate of not one world but two, school was becoming a distant third in the field of worry priorities. In fact, right now it came in a solid fourth, after fretting about the loss of Amaya.

I made my way into the kitchen, lured by the sound of laughter. The dining area was part of the massive kitchen, suiting our enlarged family to a T. I was growing accustomed to the sight of Bradley and Tara poring over vegan cookbooks, which they'd had the foresight to drag along. I hadn't even paid attention to cookware and food items, but I imagined that between our foodies and my mom, we'd manage to get enough to fill our bellies.

If not, popping out to the store to grab a few things has never been easier.

They decided on meatless chili, which we had all the ingredients for and was super easy to make, plus a massive salad with, my favorite, chocolate cupcakes with mint icing for dessert. *Yum!* Bradley and Merle flashed to the Martin's in town to grab some crusty loaves of bread, tortilla chips and salsa, and some more salad fixins.

They also picked up a few bottles of wine, so everyone could relax with a glass at dinner and we could toast our victory in freeing five of the imprisoned Perrinites—some major players at that. We'd done well.

While they was gone, Tara forced us all to take part in the dinner prep, chopping onions, lettuce, tomatoes, cilantro, celery, and carrots for the salad, plus more onions, mushrooms, and peppers for the chili. Even though the kitchen was twice the size of ours at home, we still jockeyed for position, playfully shoving each other out of the way and elbowing our way through to the silverware drawer.

Our "family" had swelled to 17 people, which created a logistical challenge even in a room this big. The dining room table, expanded to its greatest length, sat 12 people, which left five SOL. The center island was equipped with three barstools, so Bradley and Tara volunteered to eat at the counter, since they were always mucking about in the kitchen anyway.

While we chowed down, I looked around the room, and became so grateful for and appreciative of these people—for a dad I thought I'd never know, for a home and country I'd not yet seen, for teammates who'd become brothers and sisters—that I couldn't help but shed a tear. As the water worked its embarrassing way from the corner of my eye down to my left nostril, something even worse happened. . . .

You guessed it. My heart chakra started spewing a torrent of love ooze, which escaped my general vicinity and wended its way about the room, enveloping every living being and bringing along with it a general smorgasbord of verklemptitude and heartfelt professions that had been better left unsaid.

Dad lifted his glass in a toast, sounding drunk even though he was still on his first helping of wine. "I treasure each and every one of you, so much," he stopped to blow his nose. "I'm the luckiest man on two dimensions."

Oh, boy. Awkward and decidedly unkingly.

The others started to pipe up too, and there quickly ensued a laundry list of schmaltz running rampant throughout the room. *How do I rein this stuff in,* I thought, panicked.

"You're the best king EVER!"

"Your daughter's gonna rule the world!"

"I think I might be in love with Baylee," Matt blurted out.

Oh, poop.

The room quieted, people wiped the tears from their faces, and everyone looked at Matt in confusion. The green ooze slithered to the floor, where it dissipated quietly along with the lovefest.

I eyed Matt, who eyed me back, and a chair scraped across the floor as Curjan got up and left the table. I felt extremely out of sorts, but I couldn't tell if it was the inappropriate and weirdly-influenced declaration of love, or the fact that Curjan had witnessed and been bothered by said declaration.

Or was it the fact that I cared that Curjan witnessed it? *It's all so confusing.*

I'd gone from zero love interests to two in under a week. Might be a record of some kind, for me at least. Meanwhile, the logic center of my brain popped up a reminder that I had no time for ANY sort of love triangle, rectangle, or circle for that matter. I had much more important things to be doing, and I was irritated with both myself and "those admittedly hawt boys" for distracting me.

Yet the girlie part of me, the one that wanted to sit on the bed with Amaya and dish about boys and feelings and stuff, was tickled pink and yearning to get her lips or one or both of those males. *Ugh.*

As everyone else busied themselves with clearing dishes and putting leftovers away, I quietly slipped from the room, along with the good vibes that had totally abandoned our impromptu party.

I plopped onto my bed, dragging BooBoo under the covers with me for cuddles. I'd taken the smallest bedroom, which was little more than a walk-in closet, so that I could have a space all to myself. Dad and Mom had their own room, too, but everyone else was bunking up or sleeping on the living room and rec room floors or couches. It wasn't ideal, but they were soldiers and were used to slumming it as necessary. With this many people, even floor space was at a premium, yet they all took it pretty good-naturedly, at least for now.

A subdued knock at my door startled me out of my pity party, and I hesitated to respond. I really didn't want to talk to anyone right now, but I guessed I should find out who it was, at least.

"Yeah," I muttered, glumly.

"Hey, honey, it's Mom and Dad. Can we come in?" Mom's voice came through the crack in the door.

"I guess so," I replied, obviously less than enthusiastic about this new Mom and Pop development we had going on.

They sidled into the room, empathetic looks plastered on their faces. "Are you ok, honey?" Mom asked, sitting beside me and wrapping me in her arms.

"Way to make it even more awkward, Mom," I said, trying hard not to push her away, even though I was being smothered. Dad scooched onto the other side of me, and went in for the group hug.

"Ugh, guys!" I complained, secretly maybe liking it a little. I'd never had this before, so I supposed I should actually take a moment to enjoy it. I gave myself a quick pep talk about how lucky I was to have two parents who loved each other and me, and then I snaked my arms around them too, hugging them back.

My mom and I didn't really dish boy talk with each other as a general rule. She got too preachy about it, and then I got annoyed. So I typically didn't clue her into my love life, which was pretty easy given that it was usually nonexistent.

But now they had a front row seat to both my fling with Matt and my heart chakra's crush on Curjan. There was no hiding the fact that there was boy, er, man drama going on, and I didn't know whether to stall them or come clean. I mean, I wanted to have a good relationship with my parents, but I wasn't sure I wanted to have THAT good of a relationship with them.

Dad sensed my indecision, and spoke first. "Honey, I know you might not want to talk to us, given that we're your parents and all, but we want you to know we're here for you. With everything that's gone down in the past week, you're sure to be feeling completely jumbled up with stress and anxiety. Is there anything you're willing to talk to us about?"

I relented. "I'm just so confused, Dad. I like Matt, I think he's hot, sorry, and we had a great time on our first date, and then flirting and hanging around together afterward. I'm sure him blurting out that he loved me was more the influence of my poisonous love juice and insecurity over Curjan than anything else, but it still really threw me for a loop.

"We haven't been dating long enough to even think about

the L word, unless it's Lust, and that one I definitely don't want to talk to you about." I stopped to catch my breath, and continued on before I chickened out.

"And now this thing with Curjan. It's obvious that he wants nothing to do with me in that way, and I really don't want a mate either. But it hurts my feelings, still, and I can't help the way this damn heart chakra feels about it. It's almost like it's not ME feeling it, but my heart, as a separate entity. I'm attached to him but I don't understand why or how to make it stop."

I felt more miserable as I talked, pondering the entanglements between the two men.

Dad squeezed me harder, and admittedly it felt good. "Oh, baby, you know what. I would fix this for you in a second if I could, because that's what dads do, but unfortunately you're almost an adult yourself, now, so the best I can do is give you some bad advice. Then you ignore the bad advice, and wonder why you ever asked Dear Old Dad in the first place. So let's skip that whole unfortunate cycle, and I'll just say I'm here for you. Whenever you need me, whatever you need, you don't hesitate to ask. I missed out on almost 18 years, and I have a lot of making up to do." He looked at my mom. "There may be some spoiling about to go down, honey, I'm sorry. But a dad's gotta do what a dad's gotta do."

Mom smiled at him, her eyes full of the love I remembered from that first night we found Dad on the chain. Now that he'd had his say, she jumped in, too. "Who knew your dad was so smart, Bay. I think that's excellent advice, and I'll echo it. I know you miss Amaya, and usually do your girl talk with her, but I'm available to you whenever you need to talk or ask questions, honey. I know we had that birds and bees talk many moons ago, but there still may be situations that come up where you could really use Good Old Mom's advice. When that happens, I'll do my best not to be judgy judgy like you always say I am.

"I'm trying to remember that you don't 'belong' to me anymore; in fact, you never did. You're your own person, and I'm blessed to be in your life. It's my job now to catch you when you fall, prop you back up, and send you back out into the world. Just remember one thing: no one in this whole world loves you more than I do. We had no idea your future would be this challenging, but if anyone can handle it, my smart girl can. We've got your back, baby."

She gave me one last squeeze, and stood, taking Dad's hand. Before they left the room, I remembered, "Hey Dad, could you please age yourself while we have this downtime? I'd really prefer to have a dad who LOOKS like a dad, if you know what I mean."

He grinned. "Dang, I was gonna surprise you with it in the morning. Don't worry, when you wake up, you'll have that dad you've always wanted, wrinkles and all."

I grinned back. "Good luck, then, Dad! Don't get too old . . . or Mom will throw you back into the sea!"

They both laughed, and she squeezed his hand as they left the room. I hated to think about the very real possibility that she was going to have her way with that young Hawtie McHawtiepants one last time before he turned into an old dude.

Snuggling down under my comforter with BooBoo and Una, I grudgingly admitted to myself that M&D HAD made me feel a teensy bit better. *Who knew parents could do that.* I was glad I got out at least a little bit of the insanity that was all balled up in my mind and making me way cray. Although they hadn't solved my problems—no one could—sometimes just voicing the "crap" is enough to make you feel better.

I feel asleep with a tiny smile on my face. It felt sooo good to be sleeping with my babies again, and to feel somewhat safe. I needed this respite.

Something told me it would be a short one.

Chapter 15: Country Living =Da Bomb

I awoke rested and took the opportunity for a nice long stretch, for the first time in what felt like forever. I rolled over, rubbing my face on BooBoo's adorable muzzle. He meowed loudly, reminding me he probably needed to go use the litter box and get something to eat. We didn't have the luxury of our top floor kitty suite now, so I'd either need to squeeze a litter box in here with me, which was gross, or put him in the improvised cat room for hours at a time so he could eat and do his business. I got up, threw on some sweats, and carried him downstairs.

It was still early, around 7:00 a.m., but there were stirrings about the house as I ambled into the kitchen. I hoped everyone had forgotten about the unfortunate events of last evening, because I was pretty disinterested in feeling embarrassed around these people. Everyone treated me like they always did, though, and I guessed it was a good thing we had so much on our plates that my love life was of little long-term consequence to anyone.

The kitchen was soon awash in the smells of frying potatoes, and we had some fakin' bakon' in the oven, too. I could really get used to having chefs in the family, especially chefs who honored our attempts to stay meatless, egg, and dairy free out of respect for the animals who shared our planet. (Don't even get me started on the environmental consequences of it all!)

I mean, Mom and I had sometimes enjoyed making a nice dinner for two at home, but for the most part we did take out or had an "every-woman-for-herself" policy. This was a nice change.

I grabbed a cup of coffee and a seat in the corner, shutting out the world as much as I could until my first caffeine jolt of the day made me bearable. I was mesmerized by the view of the trees outside, and by the river meandering along at the bottom of the hill. I could so get used to this. I fell into a daydream, where none of this Earth-slaying existed, and I was just a normal girl (with a lot of money) who could afford this house and watch the best part of the world go by each morning with breakfast and coffee. *That would be so bomb!*

The kitchen windows and sliding doors opened up to the back deck, which was high enough off the ground that the feeling of living in a treehouse was all-encompassing. The house was surrounded on three sides by giant oak, maple, and cedar trees. I found Mom's stash of sunflower seeds and threw them off the back deck, watching as the mourning doves, cardinals, and even woodpeckers pounced on the offerings.

A squirrel popped down from a nearby tree for a bite, and an eagle flew up the river and perched on a low-hanging limb, watching for fish or other critters to capture for breakfast. Although I found him fascinating—and logically

THE CURSE OF CUR

understood the ways of the animal kingdom and that they all needed to eat—I was selfishly hoping he didn't catch anything on my watch.

Heck, I couldn't even watch those nature shows where they lions took down the gazelles. *Nope . . . no can do.*

I looked up from my musings to see Dad amble into the kitchen . . . well, I knew it was Dad, but this guy appeared different, older. His hair had started to gray along the edges, and he'd developed a slight hitch in his gate. He sported a few wrinkles, too, and his skin seemed less alive, less glowing. I laughed.

"Dang, Dad, rough night?" I called across the room.

He chuckled, calling back, "Why do you say that, Daughter? Do I look a little different this morning? Suddenly I feel like crap. If this is what getting old is, forget it! I'm staying young forever. Sorry, Honey." He playfully slapped mom on the beehive as she came in behind him, and she pinched his arm in return.

They were grossly cute.

She latched onto his arm, lacing hers through it. "No way, Dude. You're stuck getting old with me, unless you can find some way to make me immortal too. I'd be fine with that! Otherwise, I'm turning into an old lady, and there's nothing I can do about it. I'm 42 now, you look about 40; apparently my days of cradle-robbing are officially over. Now, you just have to marry me and finish the job of making us that happy family you promised over 18 years ago, Mister!" She reached up and kissed him, causing me to throw up in my mouth a little.

I mean, seriously, people. Get a room!

"Ew, Mom! Look, I'm happy we found Dad and all, and

98

I'm happy that you two are disgustingly in love . . . but not at the breakfast table. Is that too much to ask?"

She grinned at me before giving me a big squeeze. "Fine then, I'll just snuggle up to you instead, how would that be?"

"Just as gross," I mumbled, earning myself a playful pinch, too.

Soon the kitchen was full of warriors in sweats, in varying states of disarray and morning moods, and breakfast prep was in full swing. There's one thing I'd say about Bradley and Tara, they were certainly not shy about dictating to helpers and making sure everyone did their share of food prep and cleanup, which I kinda admired. Even though it meant I got roped into chopping fruit or veggies more often than not, at least I got a delish meal out of it.

When everyone had eaten their fill and was on their second or third cuppa java or tea, Dad and Charlie got down to business. I loved how they played off each other, as if they'd been doing it their entire lives, which, come to think of it, they probably had. Dad's age now resembled Charlie's, and I realized Charlie must have deliberately aged himself to look around 40 at some point as well. Hmm. I wondered why . . . what was the story behind that? I eyed him curiously; I'd obviously need to corner him to learn more about my pseudo-English friend.

"We have a lot to accomplish in these next few days, so Charlie and I have developed some suggestions, plus we want your input, too."

Charlie stepped in. "First, we need to send Samantha back to Perrin, as she's requested." He nodded at her. "But we have a lot of housekeeping to do, if we intend to quell this coup and ensure those behind it are punished. It's my suggestion that the King goes back to Perrin with Samantha, so the people can see for themselves that he's been rescued, that he's safe, and that he's more than capable of leading our world. They need to be reassured that we are the ones to follow, not the Nefarious Ninjas." Everyone smirked at my name for them, which they'd made into a joke by this point.

Whatevs. I meant that seriously, people. They obviously had no respect for a good nickname in this bunch.

"We've discussed taking Baylee back to introduce her to the people of Perrin, but we don't think she's ready for that yet. She's had very little training in using her gifts, and she needs more hand-to-hand combat training, too. We feel it would be better for her to stay here and train with Ruth and Rebecca in chakra control, and train in combat techniques and skills with Smith and Curjan. Although we know she can't attain the status of a skilled warrior in just a few days, at least she can learn how to better defend herself and take down an enemy, using the skills she has and building on them." Charlie stepped back, and King Randulf took center stage again.

"We will start some well-placed rumors about The Redeemer, as she's being called in certain circles, and the strengths and powers she's accumulating. We'll let her reputation build via word of mouth while she stays here and learns how to be all the things we're claiming she is. No pressure, Baylee, honey," he smirked at the look of horror on my face.

No, no pressure at all. Thanks, Pops.

Curjan immediately balked at staying behind, and presumably at training me. "Pardon me, King, but shouldn't I be going to Perrin with you? As your second in command, I feel it's important for me to attend all meetings with you and get up to speed on our course of action going forward, Sir. The warriors here can train Baylee while I attend with you."

I immediately felt rejected and inferior, and it pissed me off. FYI: pissed off teenager equals smartass teenager.

"Yeah, Dad, please take him with you." I flailed my arm in Curjan's general direction. "God forbid he lower himself to staying here to train me; I'm only the one who's destined to take down The Scion, at least according to the prophesy. Why would I need his help?" I huffed back down into my seat, embarrassed at my outburst.

Get ahold of yourself, Bay—apparently that man pushes my snarkitude buttons.

If I was going to be The Redeemer, then I'd need to grow skin as thick as Beelzebub—his must have been pretty thick to survive the fires of hell and all. I vowed to just treat Curjan like my dad's lackey from now on—one I needed to play it cool with and otherwise ignore, as opposed to the butthurt idiocy I'd just displayed.

I'm a dork, I decided. *Like I didn't already know that.*

Dad fixed Curjan with a stare that told him he'd brook no further argument. "As Baylee pointed out, in her inelegant way, there is no more important job than training her to take down The Scion right now. We don't yet know what powers she will gain as her remaining chakras open, but she obviously has something that the rest of us lack if she's to succeed where we had no hope. Cur, you are my highest trained and most trusted warrior. I need you to teach her as much as you can about defending herself physically and holding her own in battle. Can you do that for me?"

Cur, as Dad called him, had the good grace to hang his

head. "Yes, Sir, my apologies. I've been so focused on protecting you for all these years that I forgot our immediate mission and reverted to making you my number one priority. It won't happen again."

Satisfied, Dad moved on. "Excellent, thank you. Now, Krupert, Merle, will you be staying on with us or going back to Perrin? I know that, as leaders of the Rat and Rabbit Clans, you've been sorely missed, and probably have much to do at home."

Krupert looked at Merle before speaking. "We've discussed it at length, your Highness. Merle and I, where once we considered ourselves enemies, or close to it, have had an opportunity for much growth during our stay here. While neither of us would wish our time in captivity on anyone—except our captors themselves—we are grateful for the gift of cooperation they've given us. Most of all, this time has shown us that we genuinely like each other, and we intend to keep our friendship progressing while on Perrin, even creating joint get-togethers for our tribes so we can build an alliance and work together on the tunnel systems."

Merle spoke up. "We believe Phoebus was so successful in building an underground empire because we were not in touch with each other. We both had inklings that something wasn't right—had we shared information with each other, perhaps we'd be in a different place now. Our pride stood in the way of keeping our dimension safe, and we want to learn from that experience, do our part to protect our world. We've decided to go back, gather our people together, and talk as one. Krupert may want to rejoin you when you come back to Earth in a few days, depending on the state of his people, but I plan to stay and work from there. Rest assured you've gained two grateful and loyal generals, Your Highness, if you'll have us."

I got a little verklempt at their show of loyalty to my dad, and I begged the green ooze to stay put in my heart chakra. No one wanted a repeat of last night's performance.

Dad nodded. "That works for me, thank you gentlemen. So, to recap: Charlie, Daniel, Samantha, Krupert, Merle, and I will be heading back to Perrin as soon as I set up a secure portal with our headquarters. The rest of you will stay here; Curtis, you and Jake will get security systems and secure communications up and running. Everyone else will take turns training Baylee in your area of expertise, with the bulk of her training falling to Ruth, Rebecca, Smith, and Curjan."

Daniel interjected, speaking mostly to his team. "We'll spend three days on Perrin. While there, we'll meet with the generals of every clan and study what was learned in the interrogation of the prisoners we captured Monday night. We hope to return with supplies, troops, and a plan of action for finding that next key and the rest of the king's warriors."

The meeting broke up, and I gave myself a mental high-five. Yay! *Looks like I'm in for a good three days of physical and emotional anguish. Just what I was hoping for.*

Not.

CHAPTER 16: TRAINING DAY

Immediately implementing my "ignore Curjan" plan, I walked up to Ruth and Rebecca as soon as our assembly dissembled. I slapped a fake bright smile on my face and asked, "So, are we gonna get naked again? Good times. I'm all in."

Ruth snorted, shoving me into Rebecca. "You wish, young lady. We're just as tired of seeing your girlie bits as you are of us seeing them. If you'd stop blowing open your chakras, as a reminder, we wouldn't even need to go there! You've got three more chakras to open, so odds are good we'll be seeing you in the buff for another three sessions. Aren't we the lucky ones!

"But you're safe this morning, because we can all be clothed for these exercises. We'll go through all your chakras and relate them to the powers you already have. Then we'll go over ways in which these can be used in times of war, and how they can serve to complement your physical skills to more readily surprise and take down your enemy. Rebecca, anything to add before we get started?"

Rebecca shrugged. "Not really. We need to go to a quiet place, which isn't easy around here. For now, the downstairs rec area is being used for all training, so we'll commandeer that room and kick everyone else out to work elsewhere."

"Ok by me."

We flashed ourselves to the rec room and spent a little time tidying up, moving everyone's makeshift bedding and backpacks to the corner of the room. Now that we were down six people, though, there should be a little more breathing room for those who stayed behind. I felt a tiny twinge of guilt that I was hogging a whole room—with a bed—for myself, when the others were making do, but I pushed it aside.

Screw it. I had a feeling I was going to be a hurting pup when they were all through with me, and I'd need a place to retreat to at the end of the day to lick my wounds, aka cuddle my kitty. *I'm keeping it.*

The three of us sat cross-legged on the floor, making our own little circle. I was half nervous and half excited. I wanted to learn all I could, but I also had a healthy, or unhealthy, fear of failure, and a bad feeling I'd be failing a lot in the next few days.

Ruth and Rebecca were twins, and appeared to be of Asian descent. Both had spikey multi-toned hair, and I suspected both were gay, although that's not something I felt comfortable asking about. Ruth and Mom's bestie Janie had seemed to hit it off, and I knew for a fact that Janie was gay. That led me to believe my hunch was correct, as least as it applied to Ruth. In cat form, both women were calicos, and absolutely gorgeous.

Although known for their healing abilities, these ladies were also no-nonsense fighters, and I assumed they'd spent considerable time perfecting those abilities to make the most of their gifts in the arena.

They took turns giving me a rundown of the chakras, their associated colors, and what they were best known for. My first two chakras, called the root and sacral chakras, were already in play when we met, and weren't activated by contact with folks from my other half's dimension. The lowest chakra, red in color, was my connection to earth and tribe, and since I'd formed my own tribe with my mom, Amaya, and my animals, I'd experienced no significant difficulties or breakdowns in this area.

However, now that I had my father back and a whole new family, that dynamic would change, and it was something I'd need to keep my eye on.

We did some remedial work with the first two chakras, meditating and visualizing my connection to the earth and to my tribe. When I pictured mindlinking to the people in my group, I found that I was able to easily link with Dad— even though he'd already made it to Perrin—through the red mindtether I'd learned was for Earth-to-Perrin communications. His worried voice came through the line and into my head. "Bay, honey, everything alright there? Did you need me?"

I was embarrassed. "No, Dad, sorry. Was just working on my gifts with Ruth and Rebecca, as instructed. But hey, while I have you 'on the line', this is pretty cool that we can reach each other across dimensions now, eh? Is all ok on your end?"

"Yes. We just made it here, and I'm about to go into a meeting with Mara and Shanti, the Sorceress and the Prophetess, respectively. If anything major happens, I'll give you a ring through the tether. Until later, Daughter."

"Bye Dad," I said, a twinge of love working its way through

my body. As if on cue, a tendril of green ooze snaked out of my heart chakra, and Ruth and Rebecca immediately started laughing.

"I think that's enough for Day One," Ruth said, trying to get out of the path of the ooze of love. Rebecca scooted aside too. *No one wants any part of that particular love fest,* I smirked. "I want you to meditate again tonight before bed, because the sooner you learn to open or close your chakras at will, the sooner you can stop stuff like that from happening. But we've got to let you go meet Curjan; you're supposed to train with him at noon. Any questions?"

"Just one. Do I HAVE to go? I don't think I like that mean man," I laughed, only half joking.

Rebecca elbowed me, tittering, which seemed odd coming from either of these sisters when they seemed so no-nonsense. "We'll see how mean he is when you're finished with him. My money's on you, girl. Go get 'em!"

I was released from what would be the easier challenge of the day, and found myself with a half hour to spare before I had to meet Curjan back in the same room. I moseyed into my borrowed bedroom and crawled under the covers, looking for a few moments to hide away from the world and one man in particular. *Fine, maybe two men.*

I knew I couldn't hide forever, but I sure could hole up for 30 minutes, and I intended to take every advantage of the downtime.

Before I knew it I was out like a light, and awoke to a pounding on the door. "Wake up, Princess! Late on your first day—this doesn't bode well."

Ugh. I looked at the clock. Guess I shoulda set an alarm, but I didn't think I'd actually fall asleep. *Now this snuppity (snooty + uppity) male has one up on me. Not off to a stellar start, Bay.*

I hauled myself out of bed, ran my fingers quickly through my hair, and tied it back up in a bun and out of my face. I flung open the door, only to see Curjan leaning against the jamb, arms crossed and a scowl on his face. My heart flopped against my chest cavity (and against my will), and I mentally slammed the door shut on the ooze trying to make its way out to embarrass me. *Not today, Satan.* I smothered a giggle.

The last thing I needed was to be a walking advertisement of my reluctant feelings for the man. I was determined to get ahold of this little problem, and learn how to harness it for good instead of the evil it was currently embracing, which seemed all about shaming me and making my loved ones cry. *Weird.*

I gave Curjan a defiant look, and said "What? Can't a girl take a little beauty nap?" I was refusing to admit of course that I fell asleep by accident and hadn't set an alarm. Better to play it off like I did it intentionally. *Smart, Bay. Obviously, our working relationship is off to a fab-o start.*

"After you," he said, flourishing his arm and ignoring my show of childishness, which only served to make me feel more childish.

I strolled casually into the kitchen, getting myself a glass of water on my way downstairs. "You want anything?" I asked, trying to give off a vibe that said I didn't feel massively uncomfortable around him, and probably failing miserably. I felt conscious of every single move when he was in my vicinity, and I didn't like it. I wanted to be able to grab a glass of water without even thinking about it, which didn't seem like too much to ask. If this was mate kinda stuff, I wanted no part of it. Give me ordinary, regular love crap any day of the week.

He shook his head no, and we flashed down to the training room. I wasn't looking forward to this. Even worse, when we got there Matt was lounging against the wall, doing his best to look casual too, like he just happened to come along. His dark hair flipped and flopped, along with my heart, and he gave me his best swoonworthy smile. "Hey, Bay, how're you feeling after your earlier session? Did you get anywhere with Ruth and Rebecca?"

I shrugged. "Not really. No breakthroughs, but I have a better understanding of how the chakras interact and mesh with my gifts. That's all pretty fascinating. I never really believed in chakras before; I thought that was just touchy-feely mumbo-jumbo stuff. Now that I've realized I'm half Perrinite, and have seen the auras and how they interact for myself, I have no choice but to revise my earlier opinion. What are you doing here?"

"I thought I'd help out with your training, if that's ok with Cur," he said, looking at Curjan. "Smith's busy helping Curtis and Jake with the security system setup." He held out his hand. "What do you say? I know we got off to a rocky start when you thought I was hurting Bay, but since we have to fight this war together, we might as well let bygones be bygones and work together to make sure she's ready for what's coming."

This did not bode well. "Oh, hells to the no," I blurted, looking like more of a goof than ever. "Now I gotta make a fool of myself in front of both of you instead of just one?" I sounded whiny even to my own ears.

Curjan smirked, but then became all business. "Actually, that will be good, Matt. This way I can watch you two fight and figure out what direction we need to go in with the Princess."

I turned on him, grumpy now. "Stop calling me that!"

He held up his hands. "But you are a Princess on Perrin. Why are you acting so surly about it? I'm merely using a term of respect, the same as I use for your father."

I eyed him skeptically. "And that's all? You're not saying it mockingly? Because it sure feels like that to me."

Now he looked confused. "What do you mean, mockingly? Using your title should be the ultimate form of respect. Why would I call you Princess if I was trying to mock you?" I sighed. Obviously today's slang was lost on him.

I tried to explain. "Well, people today use the term Princess to make fun of a girl who acts like she's better than everyone else, or if they want to put her down. So I assumed that's what you were doing too, thinly-guised in formal language."

He looked taken aback. "I would never disrespect my king that way, young lady. I don't know you at all, and I understand that there's some mate talk floating around about us, but I have no intention of taking a mate, ever, and I have been trying to keep a formal distance between us so that there's no misleading impressions. I was using the term Princess as a sign of respect for both your station and my king's. What would you like me to call you then?"

I mumbled. "I guess Princess is fine, then, if you must. Or Baylee if you can handle that. But God forbid I get the wrong idea, so maybe Princess it is. Just don't say it mockingly, please."

"As you wish."

Now that the ground rules for our engagement, or lack thereof, seemed to be set, I felt a little more comfortable. I didn't yet know how old Curjan actually was, but he seemed to take his job as King's Second very seriously, and who was I to interfere with that. Plus, I was feeling less rejected now that I knew he kinda felt married to the crown . . . this would enable me to also marry myself to the crown, at least until this war was over. Meaning I could ignore both hunks of yummy hotness I was about to get handsy with. *Lordy, lordy. Dog help me.*

Curjan instructed Matt and me to try to take each other down using any skills at our disposal, even our mental powers, stopping short of actually hurting one another. He explained that when we fought the ninjas, they would be sure to use whatever dirty tricks they could against us.

I frantically tried to remember what special gifts Matt had. I knew he was weak in his flashing ability, that he could go short distances but not as far as most of the others. Maybe he wasn't as fast at I was, either, and I could use that to my advantage. I knew both he and Jake shared a similar mind ability, but for the life of me I couldn't recall what it was.

Suddenly, my mind started spinning, and I got so dizzy I thought I was gonna throw up. Before I knew what had happened to me, I was down on the floor, with Matt sitting on top of me, big grin on his face. "What the hell, Matt?" I yelled.

Now I remembered his power. Mindunwind. It made the victim's mind whirl, and if you weren't used to it, it could really throw you for a loop. As I had just illustrated, in spades.

I jumped up, the blood rushing to my face. *Kicked like a pup already.*

"Ok, Curjan, tell me, how am I supposed to guard against that happening to me? With everyone having different gifts, how can I possibly not end up on my bootie or worse, dead meat within seconds of a real war breaking out?"

"Good questions, and exactly what you need to be asking. And why your work with Ruth and Rebecca is so important. Normally we have rules on Perrin that no one uses their gifts in combat situations unless it's agreed-upon in advance. But those are the social niceties, which will not apply when we're going into a full-scale war for our world.

"Therefore, we need to teach you to guard your mind at all times, so that whatever their skillset may be, they cannot get inside and work on your mind the way Matt just did. It will be difficult at first, because you're new to fighting, and guarding your mind takes energy and focus as well. But what Matt showed you just now is the least of what will happen to you if you don't learn how to block your mind."

Matt grinned at me, squeezing my arm. "Don't worry, we'll help you get sorted out. After all, we can't let our star player go down that easily, now can we? I just wanted to give you a taste of bad-guy medicine so you'll take this seriously. For today, let's fight without mental skills; we'll bring them back in on day three. Ready to try again?"

I jumped on him in response, bringing out the tickle guns, apparently my greatest fighting asset. But this time he was ready for me, countering with a burst of rapid fire blocks and flashing behind me, grabbing my arm and twisting it behind my back. I threw myself back into him, knocking him off balance, and wrenched my arm out of his clutches. We sized each other up, playfully flashing around the room and trying to get the upper hand on our opponent.

Curjan called out suggestions while we did so, and finally stopped us to offer constructive criticism. "You two were a bit too playful for my liking, but I understand this was your first time in serious training, Princess, and you don't yet understand how far you can go without hurting your training partner. Remember, we're pretty hard to kill. Yes, we're technically immortal, but we can still die if our wounds or injuries are too severe and our bodies don't have time to heal before it's too late. So go ahead and be a little tougher on Matt. He can handle it.

"From watching you, I can see that you have some good ideas and a natural defensive posture, as well as some passable offensive moves, but you're going to have to step it up a bit. We'll spend the rest of our training today showing you counters to the moves Matt was making, and teaching you how to go on the offense, rather than playing defense all the time."

He motioned for me to move to the edge of the room, while he and Matt faced each other. Matt gave him a lazy grin, and Curjan immediately flashed to his side, threw himself to the ground, and grabbed Matt by the foot, yanking him up into the air and hanging him upside down. He laughed at the disgruntled look on Matt's face, then dropped him. He reminded me, "It's hard to expect the unexpected in hand-to-hand combat, but you've got to constantly be on your watch. I was able to surprise Matt right there because he was still in prep mode, and I went immediately into a move he wasn't expecting."

Matt huffed, and then things got a little more serious

between them. "Bring it, big boy," he taunted, eager now to show Curjan what he could do. The two settled down to some serious one-on-one, and my eyes had a hard time keeping up. Between the flashing and the speed of the hits, parries, and blocks, my eyes were about bugging out of my head. Sooner or later, in much the same way it happened when our dogs got to playing too hard, one of the men went too far, and I was growing concerned that I was gonna need backup to ensure no one ended up dead.

Finally Matt landed a hard jab to Curjan's jawline, and he was knocked across the room. Seizing my chance, I jumped between the two men, screaming "Enough! This is just getting ridiculous now. I'm not learning anything, except what buttheads you two are capable of being, which, shockingly, doesn't help me in a fight with the enemy. There's way too much testosterone in this room right now, so calm it down and let me see if anyone's injured."

They were smart enough to know not to further risk the wrath of Bay, and plopped down onto the floor, panting. Curjan had an impressive cut on his jawline where Matt's fist had landed, but it was rapidly healing. Other than that, I saw no visible injuries, so either they'd already healed or they weren't really hurting each other to the extent that it had appeared.

That reminded me of a question. "Hey, Curjan, when we were looking for the first key, we ran into and fought a batch of these ninjas. They attempted to slip a tether over my head, much the same as was used on you and your team. I was able to grab that tether, and I somehow harnessed its unique power combined with my third chakra energy, essentially turning it into a badass whip. Could I fight with that? I don't see any way I'm going to be able to learn to defend myself to the extent that I need to. Even my eyes couldn't keep up with the two of you, let alone my body. I mean, maybe with years of training, but we don't have years. However, that tether- whip thing seemed tailor-made for me. What do you think?"

He pondered. "Do you still have it? I'd like to study it and see what it's made of; maybe there is a way we can work that to our advantage."

"Yep, I brought it with me. Hold on." I flashed upstairs to my room, grabbed the tether, and zipped back down again. *Walking is so yesterday.*

Curjan studied the whip, and attempted to zing it across the room the way I had. Nothing happened. "Huh, that's weird. When I took it from that guy and used it on him, it literally zapped him like a lightning rod. Let me see it." I'd been afraid to mess with it too much, as I didn't want to end up hurting someone that was actually on my side.

I picked up the tether, which was really more like an eight-foot leash made of some kind of metallic material, and flung it toward Matt. Nothing. WTH. It had worked great for me in the heat of battle. I wondered if this was another one of those things that was useless unless I was terrified or had learned complete control of my chakra energies. *Embarrassing.*

Curjan called it a day, and asked if he could keep the tether to study a little more this evening. I felt a little uncomfortable with it being out of my sight, because truth-be-told I was counting on it to save my butt in battle, but I figured if my dad trusted him, then I should too.

"Sure," I said, "just bring it back to training with you

tomorrow, and maybe we can figure out how to use it better then. I'm beat. Thanks for the help today, guys. I'm gonna jump in the shower and grab something to eat. See you soon."

I was glad I didn't have to drag myself up the steps. Even though I wasn't as dead as I'd expected to be, today was only the beginning. The next two days would be even harder, of that I was sure.

Chapter 17: Downright Right

I hated to be proven right with regards to the 7th circle of Hades I found myself enduring in the next two training days, but my gut was shameless in its rectitude. The sessions with Ruth and Rebecca were eye-opening, to say the least, and I learned a lot about flashing control, mindlink abilities, and even my father's mindlinkslink, which I seemed to have inherited and spent some time honing. I made fun of their names for the mental abilities, but secretly I thought they were the bees knees, and did help me remember what they were used for.

The mindlinkslink was a gift very few had, and it enabled one to enter another's mind without them knowing you were there. Normally, the mindlink tethers were mentally flung out to the person you wanted to link up with. It appeared in my mind's eye as a silver string, thin and ethereal, that traveled from my headspace to that of the person I was hoping to have a little mental chat with.

Dad could sneak into most people's minds without them knowing he was there, and there was no visible tether. I had this same ability, to a limited extent so far, and I hoped with practice I could master it. Rebecca allowed me to practice on her, but Ruth got really pissy when I tried to slink in her general direction. Most people couldn't detect a good mind-linkslinker, but there were always exceptions to that rule. Ruth had a crude ability, and because I was still low-level, she saw me coming every time.

Eventually I'd get good enough that she wouldn't detect me, and that possibility seemed to fill her with fear. I grew more curious about what Ruth was hiding in that head of hers; why was she was so adamant about keeping me out? I tried to respect her privacy, because I really didn't like it when Dad and Charlie wandered around my brain either, but it still kinda nagged at me. I hoped it wasn't anything awful, like she was a spy or something. That would suck.

More than anything else, though, we practiced containing and controlling my green ooze of love—which I was thrilled about, in all actuality. I'd had enough embarrassing moments in the last few days since that chakra opened, and I really wanted to harness the ability, be in control of when or if it got used. It seemed to me that it had some very real applications in a war with the Nefarious Ninjas. Questions remained as to whether I could reach it in a high-stress situation, and if I could envelop enough of the enemy to make a difference.

There was only one way to find out, and I was not looking forward to that ultimate test.

The mental fantasy of twenty ninjas falling to the ground in tears perked me right up, though, and I chuckled as I made my way back to the training room after a light lunch. All mirth soon left me, however, when I discovered that I was alone with Curjan for training today. "Um, where's Matt?" I asked, uncomfortable. Despite the weird tension between Matt and me—and Matt and Curjan, and Curjan and me—

having him here felt like a much-needed buffer between me and the man who'd literally burst my heart open.

Curjan's mouth twisted sardonically. "Afraid to be alone with me, Princess?" he asked. "Matt's leading the rest of the team in drills outside today, as they need to get back up to speed as well. He said he'd be back for our final day of training tomorrow, so it's just us today. Rest assured, you are safe with me, so let's get to work."

We started with the dreaded calisthenics that are the bane of trainees (and teenagers) everywhere, and then progressed to hand-to-hand combat techniques. I reluctantly admitted that I was learning a lot more from this one on one time than I'd learned yesterday by watching him and Matt slug it out. I was even starting to enjoy myself . . . my gifts were starting to blend with my physical efforts after all.

Curjan had me practice blocking his abilities while he fought me, and it proved to be even tougher than I thought it would be. By the second hour I was not only mentally and physically exhausted, but drenched in sweat and dying of thirst. We took a water break, while Curjan continued in teacher mode, lecturing me on all the things I needed to do better.

Admittedly, I was thin-skinned, but I really hated being talked down to and picked at, which is what I felt was happening. "Did I do anything right, Curjan? Is that all you can do, harp on the areas I need to improve in? I felt pretty good about my progress, you jerk." I pouted and huffed to the floor, slumping against the wall.

I took my hair out of its bun, nervously running my fingers through the auburnish locks. *Pick a color, hair.* I couldn't look at him, because even though I knew I was being a brat,

I also knew that the way he was trying to teach me was not helping. I needed encouragement, and then maybe some constructive criticism, not a laundry list of all the ways I'd screwed up. I gulped back the emotions that were trying to crawl their way up from the pit of my stomach, and clamped down on the green ooze threatening to erupt with my tears.

I was doing my absolute best, *dognabbit*, and for me it was unbelievable that a mere week ago I had no idea I was anything but human. Yet here I was today, practicing ninja skills of my own, and not doing too shabby a job of it either, despite Curjan's doody-number-twody attitude.

I felt rather than saw him sit next to me, taking a big gulp of his own water. He gently poked me with his elbow, seemingly uncomfortable in the presence of an emoting woman. "Princess, I'm used to working with Perrinites, every one of whom—both men and women—have chosen to be there. By your age they've had years of practice, in what would be the equivalent of your elementary, middle, and high school grades. I recognize that your situation is very different. You're half-human and were raised here on Earth, you never knew Perrin existed, and you've never had any training. I'm doing my best to teach you as much as I can in this short period, but unfortunately there's no way we can get you up to the training level of my team of warriors in just a few days.

"The truth is you're doing amazingly well, all things considered. I know you feel awkward and clumsy, like you'll never get it, but you will. I wish we had more time, but we just don't have the years to train that you deserve. I pledge to work with you each and every day, for at least an hour, for the time we remain together, as long as you want the help. Soon things will fall into place, and I promise you, you will be amazed at what you can achieve."

I leaned against him, too tired to hold a grudge, and soaking up a little bit of his confidence and strength. We sat there in companionable silence for a few moments, and I was almost lulled into sleep. A sharp tap on my head woke me abruptly when Matt flashed into the room and broke up the solitude.

"You call this training, Bay?" He lifted a brow, and then waggled both eyebrows at me. "Get up and show me what you learned today, eh?" He glanced at Curjan, hoping for a rise.

Curjan calmly rose to his feet and ceded the floor to Matt, seemingly without a care in the world. I envied that. "Go ahead, Princess, show him what you've got."

I gave Matt a wicked grin and threw my best stuff at him, slinking into his mind without his knowledge and popping up with a "Boo" that nearly cost him the fight when he fell over backward in surprise. I doubled over laughing, and he got even with me by yanking the bun out of my hair as he flashed by, throwing the scrunchie at me from the other side of the room.

"Impressive," he conceded, although I could feel him strengthening his mental blocks, trying to make sure I didn't slip past again. "What about the tether, did you work with that today, too?"

Curjan shook his head. "Not yet, that will probably come tomorrow. I don't want her to have to rely on the tether, because if someone takes it from her, or she loses it in combat, she still needs to be able to defend herself and even go on the offensive. I think we've had enough for the day, though. I hear we're having lasagna for dinner, and I don't know about you, but I'm hungry."

"Last one showered and to the kitchen's a rotten egg!" I screamed, grabbing my stuff and preparing to flash upstairs to the closest bathroom. Both men looked at me in shock and terror, and I lost it laughing. "What, you never heard that saying before? Do you Perrinites live under a rock?" I asked.

"As a matter of fact, we live on a big rock, just like you do. What does that even mean, Princess?" Curjan was confused, and the look on his face was endearing as all get out.

"Ha, I don't really even know myself. It's just a saying we use when we want to race to do something . . . basically I was challenging you both to a race to get showered and to the kitchen to help with dinner. Ready?" Before I even finished the sentence, they were both gone, and probably in the bathroom I wanted to use, too.

"No fair!" I yelled, flashing upstairs just in time to see Curjan wink as me as he slipped into my favorite bathroom with a change of clothes.

Huh. I was surprised. *Who knew the man had a sense of humor lurking under all that analicity.*

I reluctantly gathered my things and flashed to each of the bathrooms, hoping for an empty one with a shower. I finally found one downstairs—the worst one in the house, of course—but a race was a race, and so I threw myself under the water and started soaping up, assuming at this point I would surely be the rotten egg.

Chapter 18: First Christmas

While the eleven of us who remained in the house enjoyed a delicious veggie lasagna, salad, and pumpkin spice cupcakes for dessert, we discussed the day's events and plans for Christmas, which was only two days away.

"Mom, will Dad be back in time for Christmas? I really don't want him to miss our first Christmas together as a family," I said, shoveling an extra helping of lasagna onto my plate. Since I was training so much, I was ravenous 24/7 it seemed.

"I sure hope so, honey. I was gonna ask if you'd heard from him today. I was hoping after dinner you and I could try to reach him through your mind chain, so we could ask him?"

I laughed. "Mind chain, Mom?"

"Oh, you know what I mean, Bay. What's it called again?"

"Mindlink, or tether is fine, too. You're funny."

"Well, I'm not in the know like you are, honey," she lamented. "I wish I had some kind of super powers, but alas, I'm just a human amongst gods, I fear."

I gave her a squeeze. "But you'll always be my favorite human, Mommy. So you've got that going for ya!"

"Wow, well you know what they say . . . that and two bucks will buy me a cup of coffee, eh?"

I smirked. *Mom has her moments.*

"So, everyone, are you familiar with Christmas here on Earth?" I asked the room at large.

A few nodded their heads, and it was enough to encourage me to go on. "Well, it's always been just my mom, her best friend Janie, and me at Christmas. I would so love if we could do a big family Christmas this year, since we have all the people, and a day off from our training and war might be just the tonic we need and deserve at this point. Would you all like to plan a day-long celebration of the holiday?"

Whoops and whistles were all the affirmation I needed, and even Curjan, who I suspected had a hidden stick up his bootie somewhere, agreed, with one caveat. He was kinda in command here with Dad and Charlie gone, so I was reluctantly forced to consider his input. "Ok, hit us; what's your condition?"

"As long as you tell your father when you speak to him this evening, then I won't stand in the way. If he objects, we call the whole thing off. Now, explain to us what this holiday is about, anyway?"

So I went over the ins and outs of Christmas, both from the religious standpoint and from the commercialized, but much more fun, Santa Claus perspective. We decided to exchange gifts by drawing a name from the hat, and we planned our day's menu—starting with cinnamon rolls drenched in icing—to an amazing spread with our favorite turkey substitute, mashed potatoes, stuffing, gravy, corn, and cranberry sauce. For dessert we found recipes for both pumpkin and apple pies, and would stock up on all the snacks we could stomach, too. What was Christmas without junk food and giving yourself permission to indulge, after all?

We'd need to shop for our Secret Santa gifts, but we didn't want to risk anyone being too exposed, so we decided to flash en masse to the Manassas Mall. There we split into groups of two or three to look for gifts, and then met back up to grab our long list of grocery items. Everyone stayed together as a pack in the grocery story, and we laughed ourselves silly squabbling over snacks and other goodies, everyone asking me to explain foodstuffs they'd never seen before.

Mom about had a baby cow when we rang up the $400 grocery bill, but for this many people, I thought we were getting off cheap. Besides, we'd have leftovers for a day or so at least, which was usually the best part of the holiday meal anyway.

We were all happy but exhausted by the time we got home, and Mom and I spent a little time talking to Dad through the mindlink before I fell into bed with a smile on my face, visions of sugar plums (whatever they are) and my first Christmas with both Dad and Mom—and now a ready-made extended family, too—dancing in my head.

Chapter 19: Whip 'Em Good

My elevated mood continued through Christmas Eve morning, and the others seemed more cheerful than of late, too. An air of excitement about tomorrow's holiday enveloped our guests, and I couldn't blame them…I was a sucker for Christmas myself, although it didn't go well with my grumpy teenage persona.

If it was just mom, Janie, and I, as per usual, I'd probably be sulking around today, but this year everything was different: I had a dad (finally), I had friends (a lot of them), and I was intrigued by not one but two delicious members of the male persuasion. What's not to love about this Christmas?

Aside from the impending gloom, doom, and death at the hands of Phoebus and his minions, of course. I was choosing not to think about that, though, for just one more day.

Another mood lifter for me was that I had made break-throughs in training with Ruth and Rebecca, and was finally mastering the skills that had been thrust upon me. Only time would tell if I could handle them well enough to protect myself and others while taking down the bad guys, but my confidence level had gone up a level or three.

I was nervous about training with Curjan today, because

we were finally going to work with my makeshift whip, and given that I hadn't succeeded in getting it to respond to me again, another massive failure loomed. I shoved that fear aside, too, refusing to allow negativity to sabotage me before I even got started, and went outside on the deck to soak in the calming vibes of the flowing river and fresh air.

The air was crisp and clear, but the forecast called for a slight skiff of snow after midnight. I could think of no more perfect way to spend Christmas with my new family . . . two fireplaces crackling, hot chocolate, games, delicious food, and then more snacks for good measure. Perhaps a Marvel movie marathon was in order, too, which I felt pretty confident the team would LOVE.

I took one last look at the amazingly peaceful river view and flashed myself to the training room to face the music. As soon as I appeared Curjan attacked me—in a surprise move that I fully expected—because why wouldn't he on our last day? Oh, and my gut warned me . . . dead on, as usual.

I easily evaded his attack and responded with some quick punches and an attempted mindbind—which would have knocked him out—but his mental block held firm. I got a grudging nod of approval for my efforts, however, which was better than the previous day. I'd take it.

We sat down to study the whip together, and he told me what he'd been able to piece together so far. "I'll to start at the beginning, since I'm not sure how much you know; is that amendable to you, Princess?"

I nodded, and he continued.

"When your father, Samantha, the rest of the pack, and I were attacked and captured in our canine forms in the wilds of the Shenandoah Mountains, we were taken to a facility somewhere off the grid, where we were confined and tortured. Because the entire pack had already gone feral as a result of the curse placed upon anyone who, er, copulated with a human, we were out of our minds to begin with, and had no understanding of what was happening to us.

"Just to be clear, here, Baylee, your father was aware he would be cursed and would turn to his feral shepherd counterpart for having relations with your mother. He had willingly given up his life as king in order to save our realm, because you were divined as our only chance to save our dimension. What he didn't know—and we still don't understand why except to theorize that it was because our bond with him was so strong—was that the whole pack would go feral with him. Are you with me so far?"

I nodded again, kinda' glad we were started at the beginning so it was all fresh in my mind. "Yeppah, gotcha so far, Cur," I giggled, although why I did that I would never know—it seemed neither the time nor the place for such flippancy. Next I'd be twirling my hair with my fingers. *Curse these female hormones!*

He eyed me quizzically, but moved on. "We'd gone for a pack run in the Shenandoah Mountains, ecstatic about your mother's pregnancy and our hopes to save Perrin, when the curse struck the pack as a whole, turning us all feral simultaneously. I remember my mind slipping, and one brief moment of understanding of what was happening to me, before it all turns to a blur in my mind. It's hard to explain what it's like to live as a feral dog, but just try to picture how any wild animal might live. We were closest to wolves at that point, so we lived as wolves might; we hunted and ate as one, we shared basic communication via mental images through the pack mind, and settled in to a very simple life. We knew nothing else.

"Because that time is such a blur, I have very few memories of what occurred after we were captured, which I suppose I should be grateful for. One of the few things I DO remember, though, involves them fitting me with a collar and chain made from the same material as this." He picked up the "whip", a look of anger and humiliation on his face. "The collar was attached into the base of our skull, and it was the most painful experience of my life, bar none. I shrieked in pain, and I remember hearing others in the pack shrieking, too. They used that device and chain to control us, with the collar locked into place so it couldn't be easily removed. Then the chain was hooked up to a ground stake, at least once we were dispatched as guard dogs in the field, which linked to their equipment and kept our minds fuzzy and any of our past memories blocked."

"So how was I able to use this as a weapon, then, do you think?" Truth be told, I was growing a little impatient with the history lesson and wanted to skip to the good stuff. *Let's move it along, here, dude.*

He chuffed at me, still in dog mode, and I tried not to snort out loud. *Snickering in my mind, buddy.* "I'm getting there, Princess. So this leash must have some of the properties of the mindlink tethers that are the hallmark of our society. Everyone communicates via tether, as least as often as we talk out loud. Every Perrinite can, in essence, ring the mind doorbell of another Perrinite, and if accepted for communication, can talk back and forth that way. Most block much of their brain from intrusion by others, for obvious reasons. Let's just say we all keep a 'front porch' in our minds where we receive guests, and 'visit' with them there, while the rest of our mind resides behind a closed door. Does that help you understand a bit more about how the tethers operate?" he asked.

"Yeah, Ruth and Rebecca explained it in a similar way, and since I can now do it myself, I get what you're saying. But how are those principles manifested in the actual chain, or leash in this case? That I haven't yet been able to understand."

"I think they first developed the seeds of this technology over 20 years ago, before we were imprisoned, and they have been perfecting it ever since. They take our innate and inborn gifts of mindlinking one step further, by infusing the chainlinks with technology that mimics the mind tether and overrides the ability to accept or reject a request to connect. Basically, the chain forcibly connects to your mind and allows them to overtake it. At which point they are in control—and that's they have been implementing mindblocks and mindswipes on our citizens."

The lightbulb finally went off in my head, and I understood the power of what we were up against. "Gotcha. So why am I no longer able to link up with this thing, then?" I touched the tether.

"Here's my theory. The day you in essence turned it into a whip . . . that ninja was trying to place it over your head, so it was activated, right? He was planning to capture you and overtake your mind with it, allowing him to take you without a fight."

"Yeppah, at least that would make sense, so I guess so."

"But you grabbed hold of it before he had it in place, and, by it connecting with your third chakra energy, zap him into oblivion instead. I don't think they expected that or were prepared for it. Which makes me believe you are manifesting a gift the rest of us don't have, and it's related to these tethers. I believe you—and only you at this point—can overcome the power of their leashes and chains when you learn how to harness your gifts. You did it that day out of desperation and sheer fear-filled adrenaline. But today, we will explore how you can connect up with it again under your own power and control, making you a force to be reckoned with. If you can overcome this technology which they plan to use to enslave our people? You can save us all."

He sat back, proudly patting himself on the back for figuring out how and why I could make myself useful as this so-called Redeemer. Which was all well and good, theoretically, and it was actually the first viable theory I'd heard, but since his hypothesis had yet to be proven in the lab, aka the training room, I wasn't sure what he was strutting on about.

Men. They do one little thing and suddenly they're God's gift to humanity. Or immortality. Snort.

We stood up, and Curjan and I walked through what happened that night, to the best of my remembrance. The ninja had rushed up behind me, and Charlie had shouted a warning just in time. As he began to slip the tether over my head, I grabbed it, screamed in rage, and then the thing had turned "live", zapping him and tossing him back into the wall. I then kept the tether in hand, clumsily using it as a whip on the next ninja, which zapped her into unconsciousness, too.

I remembered an overwhelming sensation of yellow throughout, like everything was awash in it, so I believed it likely that my third chakra had linked up to the tether and created the current.

"Alright, then, let's first work on learning how to handle the whip when it's not electrified." We spent the better part of an hour working on drills and techniques for cracking the leash like a whip, using it as a lasso, and swinging it to knock the legs out from under an opponent or inflicting some heavy-duty damage on the upper body.

"One thing we have on our side right now," Curjan said thoughtfully, "is that the two ninjas you zapped through the tether are in our custody. As long as we don't have a spy where they are being held and questioned, they haven't yet been able to tell Phoebus or his men that you can manipulate their mindcontrol tether. This will give us the element of surprise, and hopefully put a real damper on their plans moving forward."

When we were both satisfied that I'd gotten a handle on manipulating the whip without any special powers, we moved on to attempting to energize it.

I tried and tried, pretty sure I was making that embarrassing constipation face, *awkward*, as I attempted to push the energy from my third chakra to the leash, but nothing was happening.

Cur gave me a calculating look, then mumbled, "I'm sorry for what I'm about to do, Princess," and then he grabbed the tether and wrapped it twice around my neck.

He wasn't playing, though, this time, and he began squeezing until I was afraid I was going to die—my eyeballs were about to pop out of my head! *I can't breathe!* I screamed inside. I tried to vocalize, to call out for help, but my throat was blocked and I felt death inching nearer with each passing second. It was a horrid and helpless feeling, and then suddenly a wash of powerful rage unleashed and worked its way up my body, from my toes all the way to the top of my head.

I recalled how Rebecca and Ruth had taught me to use that whoosh of energy when I found myself in an emergency situation, so I forced open my solar plexus and shoved the yellow energy from that area. In a flash it encircled my body and zipped its way into my hands—and by extension the leash. Curjan bucked as the energy jumped from the leash into his body and he released the tether, slumping to the ground, knocked out cold.

At that moment, I could've cared less about the state of his health. I rolled over, choking and sputtering, and pulled the noose from my neck, tossing it to the side. I was all but still out of it, waiting for breath to slowly eke its way back into my lungs. My neck hurt something fierce, and I knew I'd have one hell of a bruise tomorrow.

Excellent Christmas present, Cur, thank you so much. Oh, maybe I'll live after all—snark present and accounted for.

I doubted that Dad and Matt were going to appreciate Curjan's tactics—I know I sure didn't—but I was grudgingly beginning to understand that he did what he had to do to force my powers to surface. In his defense, I knew we'd tried everything else we could think of, without success. If this was indeed my special power, we had no choice but to bring it into existence, using any means necessary. *Ouch.*

While I wasn't sure I'd forgive him anytime soon, as a burgeoning warrior I knew that sometimes shitty things had to happen in order for good to fight evil. If they were tough, we had to be tougher.

I crawled over to him, placing a hand on his chest. *Good,*

he's breathing, at least. Although it does seem a little shallow . . . poopsicles.

I pushed him, rocking his body back and forth. "Curjan? Curjan! Wake up, dude. Are you ok?"

He opened one eye, studying me. "Ugh. Everything hurts, Princess. I guess it worked, huh? Now I know how those traitors felt when you zapped them. That's a mighty powerful weapon you have, I'll give you that. I'd be excited if I weren't still half-dead."

He slowly rolled onto his side and propped himself up on a still-quaking elbow. "I'm very sorry that I hurt you, Baylee. Please accept my apology. I didn't know any other way to make it happen other than to force you into a position where you had to open up in order to save yourself. You're already starting to bruise." He brushed his hand across my neck, and my heart almost lost it, the beat becoming frantic with a need I spent every minute of every day denying. I looked up at him, my feelings surfacing and pooling into my eyes.

"Princess, don't look at me that way," he pleaded, as if the look in my eyes awoke a matching need in him. "I've made a vow to remain unattached as part of my duty to king and country. The last thing either of us needs is any kind of emotional entanglement." He brushed his lips against mine, belying the words that had just sprung from his mouth, and I leaned forward, hoping for more.

And that's when Matt popped by for a visit.

Chapter 20: Speaking of Entanglements

"Matt!" I screeched, rolling backward and springing to my feet. *Gah, guilty much, Bay?*

"Um, what's up?" I wrung my hands, trying to sound innocent and flirty.

It was lame, and I knew it. To be drooling over one man who my heart craved one second, and then bending over backward to keep another man interested the next was ridiculous and beneath me. *Lame. Just lame,* I chastised myself.

Matt went with the avoidance route, *Thanks be to Dog,* which was smart given that we didn't need another brawl on Christmas Eve. "Hey, Bay," he flirted back. "I thought maybe you'd want to go with me out to the woods and get some fresh cuts of pine to decorate the living room. Your mom and a few of the others popped back to your house to get the Christmas tree and ornaments and bring them over. We're starting to get into party mode, and I thought it'd be nice for us to get away for a moment?" He batted his long, sexy lashes at me, and I immediately melted.

"Sure, I'm in. Let me grab a coat and some boots first, though." I turned to Curjan. "Thanks for helping me understand why I couldn't access the whip. Hopefully such extreme measures will never be needed again, right?" I laid a hand on his arm, seeking to reassure both of us. "Please don't feel bad about what you did. It probably was the only way."

I gave him a soft smile and flashed to my room, but not before I caught a glimpse of Matt throwing a triumphant grin in Cur's direction, and Curjan returning a look that spoke volumes.

Oh, for the love of river otters. This testosterone-laden tension was both exciting and annoying at the same time. Usually it was just plain old irritating—yet there was an embarrassingly feminine part of me that couldn't help but feel a little bit stoked that two men were interested.

For the millionth time, an overwhelming need to talk to Amaya took hold; except now I couldn't even check my phone to see if she'd texted, since our phones had been con-fiscated by Curtis and Jake before we left my house. Their justification was that the F of N's (Foul Faction of Nefarious Ninjas, lest you forget) could track our phones and know exactly where we were.

Yeah, yeah, yeah.

I got that they did that on TV all the time, but still, your average bad guy wasn't that good and didn't have access to the necessary hacking equipment, right? Yet the responsible side of me knew it was better to be safe than sorry, and these particular bad guys were probably crossing their T's and dotting their I's. My gut was adamant that we'd be in grave danger if they figured out where we were, so I grudgingly accepted my phoneless existence.

Jake had provided me with a burner phone, but who was

I gonna text? They could be monitoring Amaya's phone too, so if I wanted to keep her safe it was better to keep her out of it altogether.

Would it really hurt just to pop into her bedroom tonight to tell her Merry Christmas?

The devil on my left shoulder put the idea into my head, and the more the idea festered, the better it seemed. The angel on my right shoulder begged and pleaded, though, for me to think about it for awhile longer.

Fine, till tonight, I told the angel, all the while at work on my own nefarious schemes. I gave her my most beatific smile, and a fake nod of acquiescence.

Happier now that I had a plan, I threw on my jacket, hat, boots, and gloves, *(it's cold out, man)* and met Matt at the front door. "Ready, cutie?" he said, tweaking my hat with his fingers in a gesture of intimacy. I suddenly felt uncomfortable—excited, guilty, and most of all very, very confused. I wanted to be happy flirting with Matt again, and a part of me was still really attracted to him. He was fun, sexy, and he made my heart go pitter patter. What was so wrong with that? I wasn't even 18 yet, for flip's sake!

Determined to push all thoughts of Curjan from my mind, I threw Matt a cheeky smile. "You betcha, hot stuff. Pine cones and cedar branches and holly, here we come!" We grabbed a pair of clippers and tromped off into the woods, just as it started to flurry.

The further we got from the house, the more the quiet and the freedom of the moment brightened my mood. I twirled, arms flying, head thrown back, and peals of laughter escaped my chest. I loved snow, and especially snow at Christmas!

Matt laughed too, grabbing me up and twirling me in his arms until we'd both grown dizzy. He stopped, holding me aloft, and brought his cold nose to mine. He gazed deeply into my eyes, grinned wryly, and set me down again. He spotted our target, took my hand, and pulled me along to the nearest holly bush. My eyes widened, taking in the full extent of this thing—*holy crap, it's almost 20 feet tall!*

We snipped carefully and took only as much as necessary—I was all about treating our planet with kid gloves—just a few luscious sprigs for the hearth. Then we added pine boughs, tossed some cones in a bucket for decoration, and clipped some cedar trimmings, too.

I just couldn't wait until tomorrow!

Dad would be home then, and I could picture the sight and smell of all the delicious food, the warm glow of the fire, and the underlying scent of pine wafting through the house. Heavenly.

When we'd collected all we could carry, we popped ourselves back to the living room, setting it all down on the rug. Mom was already back and snoopervising the tree trimming, grabbing me up in a delicious mom-hug. I snuggled down into her arms. *I've missed this.*

"My baby!" she cried. "How was your afternoon, honey? I haven't seen you all day! I think Dad's coming home soon!" Her excitement was contagious, and I jumped up and down with her, hugging it out. Between the almost-kiss with Curjan, the almost-kiss with Matt, the snowfall, living in this dream home, and Christmas being tomorrow, I didn't think I could get any happier.

Well, there is one way. The devil on my shoulder was back, reeling me in with just one word: *Amaya.*

I left the gang happily squabbling over where to put the woodland décor, and took myself off to the shower. Once in the buff I examined my neck, and was relieved to see that most of the bruising had already healed. It appeared I had myself a dose of Perrinite healing genes after all, and I'd never be angry about that. The last thing I wanted was to face an inquisition about why my neck was injured, and have Curjan questioned about his training techniques.

I dug out my favorite white scarf and wrapped it around my neck, pairing it with my cozy and warm burgundy sweater and skinny jeans. I found my sterling cat earrings and my faux doc martins, and took a quick look in the mirror, loving the way my hazel eyes sparkled and my almost-auburn hair waved to just past my shoulders. I was feeling kinda good about myself right now, and it showed.

I arrived back in the living room just in time for the transformation to be unveiled: Christmas lights wrapped around each of the sliding glass doors, our 8-foot tree nestled between them on the far wall, and my beloved ornaments from childhood snuggled deep within her branches. Everyone oohed and aahed, and we set to work building little mini pizzas for our Christmas Eve dinner, a tradition Mom and I had started when I was but a wee lass.

The TV played soft Christmas music in the background, and we all joked and laughed together as we cooked in the kitchen. The man of my dreams, aka my dad, popped into view, and Mom shrieked, throwing herself into his arms. I kinda thought my heart might explode, too! It was a testament to my lessons with Ruth and Rebecca that I managed to keep the green ooze from spilling everywhere with this much love circulating my body and the room.

I gave Charlie a big hug; I hadn't realized how much I'd missed him, or that I truly was starting to look on him as the uncle I never had. In fact, I was afraid I actually loved the man, and I gave him a tighter squeeze. He held me at arm's length, popping into my head for a private conversation. "Well, hello, beautiful! You look ravishing, and so happy. Living out here agrees with you. Anything I need to know?"

I smiled, noticing his eyes looked more weary than usual. "I've learned so much in the last few days, Charlie. Your team is amazing, and Ruth and Rebecca helped me control the green ooze, so thank you. More importantly, what do I need to know about what went down in Perrin?"

"Let's save that topic for after our Christmas celebration, shall we? I think we're all in need of a little break, and things were pretty heavy up there. For now, let's enjoy this beautiful country home and the company of those we most love at this special time of year. I haven't gotten to celebrate Yuletide since my days in Europe so many years ago. I grow nostalgic just smelling the pine and the fireplace, and seeing the twinkling lights." He gave me another squeeze, and I rested comfortably in his arms. *So this is what it's like to have an amazing uncle. Unimaginably delicious!*

I greeted Daniel, who'd come back with Dad and Charlie, and soon the party was in full swing, with food, fun, frolic, and even some spiced cider and wine for those able to handle adult libations. Even though Mom and Dad probably would have let me have a glass, I didn't feel I was in any emotional position to handle alcohol right now anyway, so I settled for laughing at the others who had a little too much to drink.

Ruth flashed into town to pick up some more wine and

came back with Janie on her arm, and another wave of revelry rippled through the room. Mom and Janie were thrilled to see one another, and high fives and shouts of "Yay, Janie's here" could be heard around the room. When I was finally able to get a word in edgewise, I grabbed her and snuggled up to my "second mom", watching everyone with a big smile on my face.

An hour later, I was gently shaken awake by a concerned Curjan, asking "Princess, are you feeling well? I grew concerned since you were injured today that you could be worse off than we realized."

I yawned and stretched. "Nope, Cur, no worries. I'm fine, actually, just sleepy and full. I think I'll call it a night. And, on the bright side, my neck was almost healed by the time I'd showered, so I must have gotten Dad's super-healing gene! I'm stoked about that. Night, Curjan. Merry Christmas." I lightly touched my hand to his, and he, seemingly unconsciously, gave my fingers a quick squeeze before releasing.

"Night, Princess. Merry Christmas to you, too."

Chapter 21: Uninvited Guest

Now that I'd had a nap, brushed my teeth, and tucked myself into bed with my untrusty sidekicks BooBoo and Khronos, I found myself wide awake and staring at the ceiling. The argument between the little devil on my left shoulder and the angel on my right raged on with regards to the wisdom of popping in for a visit with Amaya.

If I'd been as sleepy as I was earlier, the angel would have won by dint of an immediate lapse into slumber, but since I was now wide-eyed and bushy-eyebrowed *(what, I need a pluck!),* I was ripe for trouble.

And it *was* Christmas Eve . . .

I *ALWAYS* saw Amaya on Christmas Eve. Her family life kinda' stunk, and they didn't really care if she was home even on the night before Christmas, so she always hung out with me at Mom's and we exchanged our gifts then.

I'd picked up a shirt that screamed "Amaya" on our shopping excursion the other day, and even wrapped it before going to bed. *Really, what would be the harm in me just dropping by to give it to her?*

The devil's argument was most compelling.

Thank you, demon. Lordy, I was losing it.

I was wearing my favorite Christmas jammies, and since

I'd be going directly from my room to hers, I left them on— maybe they'd soften her up. We'd sported matching jammies for the past three years, and maybe, just maybe, she still loved me enough to be wearing hers too.

Only one way to find out. I was nervous, truth be told.

Amaya was REALLY angry at me. Like super angry. And the Wrath of Dog had nothing on the Wrath of Amaya.

One of the arguments made by the angel was that if I went to see Amaya, I'd be forced to come clean. She wouldn't tolerate any less. I couldn't lie to her anymore and expect to stay her friend.

But if I told her the truth, I'd be putting her in danger.

It was a dilemma.

I selfishly wanted, no, NEEDED, my best friend. And if the scenario was reversed, and she was suddenly half-Perrinite and had to fight an epic war against Nefarious Ninjas *(she at least would appreciate my nickname)* I'd want to know about it and be part of her life, regardless of the danger.

It was the right thing to do, after all.

So I slipped out of bed and to the bathroom for a hair check, throwing on a little lip gloss for the special occasion and checking my breath. Then, clutching my gift to her in both hands so I didn't somehow lose it along the way, I threw out a mental tether directly to Amaya's room, and yanked.

It was my first time trying to go any distance, and I could feel myself whoosh through the air, blindly praying I'd wind up in the right place. How awkward would that be if I plopped down in some stranger's house in my Christmas jammies? *Oi.*

Within seconds I'd landed in Amaya's room and fell onto the bed, the gift flying out of my hands. *How flippin' long*

THE CURSE OF CUR

does it take to learn how to arrive in style?

I looked around the room, but there was no Amaya. *Where is she?* I checked the clock, and it was dead on midnight. Surely she'd be in bed by now. I snuck to her door and opened it just a crack to take a peek out into the hallway. Voices raged downstairs, and then Amaya came stomping up the steps, pain written all over her face.

Ugh, yet another fight with Stepmobster Robin. I hate that woman.

I pitied Amaya for having to live with such a mean and nasty creature. I pitied myself too, because now that she was in a more craptastic mood, I had a sneaking suspicion that I was about the bear the brunt of some serious tongue-lashing.

I squared my shoulders and crept quickly back to the bed, preparing myself for Amayageddon.

She stormed into the room, slamming the door shut behind her. It took her a moment to realize I was there, huddled on her bed, clutching my gift.

As soon as she saw me she broke down, sobbing, and ran into my arms, shoving the gift to the side and hugging me as if she'd never let go. I was verklempt too, now, so I went ahead and sobbed with her, making sure the green ooze hadn't somehow escaped my heart chakra and overcome us both.

Nope. Just pure, old-fashioned bestie love.

When we'd gotten ahold of ourselves to the point of mopping up the tears and looking awkwardly about the room, I started. "I'm so sorry, Amaya, that I wasn't honest with you and have been blowing off spending time together. I want to tell you everything now, so we don't break up ever again. I don't like my life without you in it. It doesn't make sense to me."

She nodded, blowing her nose. "I feel the same way. After just getting into it with the Stepmudder again, all I could think as I stormed up the steps was that I needed you back in my life. I need your shoulder to cry on, I need you to laugh with, hells, I just need you, Bay. I've never in my life been so happy to see you! Yay!"

We both fell out laughing, giggling and rolling on the bed. She grabbed the gift I brought her and dug one out from under her bed, wrapped too.

We giggled conspiratorially as we opened them, ecstatic that, while we were so different in looks and temperament, we were alike in the ways that really mattered; and that— even in the middle of a friend-breakup—we'd still bought each other Christmas gifts. That was love.

Afterward, Amaya grew serious, pointing a finger at me and giving me "the look" that meant I was still in deep doggy doodoo after all. "You've got some splainin' to do, my friend. Let's hear it." She crossed her arms and waited.

Ugh, where do I even start? At the beginning, Bay. At the beginning. It was gonna be a long night.

"Ok, well, remember the day we got sent to the principal's office for refusing to dissect cats?"

"Duh, yeah, of course. That was the beginning of whatever's-been-going-on-with-you, and I've been over it a million times trying to figure out what in Hades happened."

I held my right hand up to God. "I swear I'm gonna tell you the whole truth, and nothing but the truth, but you've got to hear me out, and try to believe me. It's super far-fetched, but every milligram of it's the truth."

"O . . K . . . then. Go."

"That day, as we sat in the principal's office, a voice came into my head, and he sounded like a 40-year-old British dude. I was freaking out, looking around and trying to figure out what was going on; and then the whole school exploded into mass mayhem. I assume you've heard tales of the cats in the biology lab coming back to life and chasing the students through the halls, right?"

"Yeppah . . ." she rejoined, and I smiled. We both popped our p's on "yep", and I missed that so much. The grownups just didn't get it.

"Well, turns out it was one of those cats that was talking to me in my head."

Amaya's jaw literally flew open.

"Get the flip out of here!" she whisper-screamed. I laughed.

"I know, right? . . . and no more interruptions. Let me just get the whole story out." She made the lip-zipping motion every girl learns in grade school.

I launched into the long and involved tale of the last week, leaving nothing out, Amaya's eyes growing bigger by the second.

It was a half-hour before I finished up. "So, the reason I've been avoiding you is that I didn't want you to get hurt. These are very, very dangerous people, who mean serious biznatch when it comes to taking over both Perrin and Earth. If something happened to you I'd never forgive myself, and that's why I feel so weak for even coming here now. I've been so, so torn." I grabbed her by the hand and held on for dear life.

"I missed you more than you'll ever know. But not telling you was the only way I knew of protecting you. Getting you involved could kill you and that would kill me. Can you forgive me for both not telling you before and for dragging you into it now?"

I'd never witnessed Amaya speechless before, but she simply sat, tears rolling down her face. "I'm so grateful you're here, babe." She grabbed me up in a girlie hug, one that doesn't let up for like three hundred seconds. "Although this is some majorly effed up shiz, it's actually better than the thought that you just didn't love me anymore, you know? And I'd rather know everything that was going on with you, even if it puts me in harm's way, than be left in the dark, alone and lonely without you."

Now the tears were pouring down my face again, too. "I know! I hated that I was making you feel like I didn't care. It was just the opposite, actually. I finally realized, if the shoe were on the other foot, I'd rather know and be part of your life than be protected and feel left out. So here I am, warts and all." I shrugged.

She perked up, winking at me saucily, and—just like that—the old Amaya was back. "So, two boys, huh? Nevermind the end of the world stuff. I'm more interested in the Matt and Curjan deets. Who's yummier? Now I get why you got so huffy when I was flirting with that boy. Not my fault—you told me he was your cousin! That's on you, my dear.

"And the sexy thang that picked you up from school the other day? That was your *dad*?" She exploded in laughter, and we both rolled around on the bed giggling again. I mock-shuddered.

"Yeppah. And you'll be happy to know that he's now aged

himself to look fortyish. Not that you won't still drool over him, but at least he actually looks like a dad now. That was merely ONE of the many traumas I suffered this last week." I dramatically put my hand palm out to my forehead and fell over backwards.

"So, you didn't answer the question of who's tastier—Matt or Cur?"

"Oh, man, they're both hawt. Supa hawt. Like Matt has that pretty boy thing goin' on, which you know. Dark, shoulder-length curls, long lashes, dark brown eyes. And he really works it. He's a born flirt, which I can respect, but it makes me a bit leery of trusting him if we were to get into an actual relationship. He makes my heart flutter, though, there's no doubt about it." I put my finger to my lips, thoughtfully.

"On the other hand, Curjan wants no part of a relationship, or even a flirtation. He's all business, all the time, and thinks only of protecting the king, i.e. Dad, and I guess the king's family, i.e. Mom and I, to a limited extent. I believe he's just as drawn to me as I am to him, but he pushes it aside, covers it up. Which makes it easier for me to do the same, but I will confess that it kinda hurts my feelings, too."

"Yet," I said uncertainly. "I really should be focusing on the whole 'saving of the worlds', you know? I shouldn't be dreaming about boys for even one second right now. I'm kinda disgusted with myself that I am . . . but I *AM* a teenage girl, and we both know I like me some boys," I giggled. "What do you think?"

"Ugh," she said. "How can you possibly choose? I mean, though, if you think Cur is your mate, how can you even consider giving Matt a chance? Shouldn't you wait and see how things play out with Curjan first?"

"Well, there's honestly nothing to play out. I mean, yeah, we had that brushing of the lips, which was to die for . . . and I don't know if it would have been more if Matt hadn't popped in at that exact moment. But I feel rejected by Cur, big time, and so that makes me want to run into Matt's arms, if for no other reason than to show him. And, before you ask—yes, the adult part of me realizes that's no way to handle it, and no reason to date poor Matt, just to piss of Curjan? So, you're right, as usual. I guess."

I'm confused, dognabbit!

We hung out awhile longer, talking and giggling, and snuggling up under the covers, but in just a platonic best-friendsy kinda way. We'd really missed each other, and I was so, so happy to have my soulmate back. As the clock struck 2:00 a.m., I reluctantly got up to leave. I let her know I'd be in touch as soon as I could, but reminded her that NO ONE could know a word about this, and to be very careful about the boys she flirted with. If new boys showed up at school or in her general vicinity—and they were supa good-looking—she had to promise me she'd RUN the other way, because they were most likely playing for Team Nefarious Ninja.

Having sworn on our renewed friendship—and against all her basic flirtatious instincts—that she'd take this all very seriously, it was time for me to take my leave.

Giving her one last hug and longing for some kitty-lovin's, I flashed myself back to my bedroom—only to be greeted by a furious Mominator and her new trusty side-kick, the Dadinator.

Uh oh. So much for catching a few zzzzz's before Christmas morning. Looks like I'm in for Round Two of Beat On Bay.

Chapter 22: Christmas Cheer

Faking good cheer to throw Mom off the scent, I pulled out my biggest grin. "Hello, Madre! Imagine meeting you here. Merry Christmas! Feliz Navidad," I threw in for good measure, hoping my grasp of the Spanish language would impress her.

Her eyes told me in no uncertain terms she wasn't falling for it. *Not today, Satan,* they opined, and I stifled laughter behind a cough.

"What's up?" Like teenagers the world over, I was a fan of pushing boundaries whenever I could, and since she still hadn't spoken, I figured there was no harm done in continuing the innocent act.

"Cut the crap, Baylee Marie." *Uh oh. She pulled out the middle name—RUN.* "Where have you been? Your father and I have been worried sick." *That phrase comes with every parenting manual.*

"Um, I had a little last minute shopping to do, so I flashed out to the mall."

"At midnight?"

I shrugged defensively. "There are stores open all night on Christmas Eve, hoping for last minute shoppers like me."

"Then where are your bags?"

"Oh." *Shoulda' thought that through.*

Dad stepped in. "Before you embarrass yourself further with this charade, Baylee, I need you to know that I placed a tracker of sorts in your mind. Very few people know I can do this, and so this information needs to stay between us. I'm able to track up to five people at a time by slipping an unseen tether link into your mind— kinda like those tiles you all put on your phones and purses in case you lose them."

Oops. Did not know that. The jig's up.

I flounced over to my bed and threw myself down, pouting now that I was found out and looked like an idiot in front of my dad. "Then I guess you know where I was, so why bother asking?"

"I was checking if you'd lie to me, Baylee, and I'm disappointed to see that you did. Why?" asked Mom, hurt showing in her eyes.

"Well, I knew I wasn't supposed to tell Amaya our secrets, but I couldn't take it anymore. It's Christmas, and I missed my best friend. How would you feel if you couldn't tell Janie what was going on with you? Amaya thought I didn't love her anymore, and she was hurting." I lifted my chin. "I told her everything."

Mom's face relaxed, and fell into a look of resignation. "I figured as much. I know that was hard for you, honey, but we were just trying to protect her from harm. Now you've made your decision, and we will all have to live with the consequences."

She squeezed me tight. "Did she forgive you at least?"

I rolled my eyes. "You know Amaya. She was more concerned with all the male juju going around over here than the bad stuff about to befall two dimensions. I love that girl."

I sighed. "But at least she feels better now, and she's promised to keep our secrets. I told her I'll contact her when I can, but for now we're 'in hiding', and she understood. Plus we exchanged gifts . . . check out the new shirt she bought me! Pretty cool, eh?"

Mom did the obligatory oohing and aahing, and Dad sat down on my other side, pulling me in for a hug, too. "Well, Bay, we'll do our best to keep her safe. I'm glad you have your friend back, even though I'm not onboard with how it happened. Just so you know, I'm not removing the tracker from your mind. You're in too much danger. Hopefully the Eff of En's can't find it or block it, and this way if anything happens to you we'll be able to find you."

Knowing that actually gave me a little peace of mind, and since I wasn't in the habit of running off to do drugs or whatever, I didn't have much to hide from the parental units anyway. I could live with it—at least until we destroyed those nasty ninjas, and I got my life back. Then we'd have to renegotiate those boundaries.

"That works for me, Dad, for the time being at least. Thanks. Do you think I'll be able to do that too?"

"Well, you've still got three chakras to open, and usually, in someone as powerful as you're turning out to be, more gifts will be released with each activation. So maybe."

"That would rock. I'd keep one on both of you and Amaya, so I'd never lose the three most important people in my world." I hugged them, and then pushed them away. "Now, what does a girl need to do to get a little beauty sleep around here? I want to be lookin' dapper when I open my first ever Christmas gifts from my Dad, so you better get to wrapping, Santa, while I catch a few winks."

Dad got a panicked look on his face and dragged Mom out of the room. I smirked. *That oughta keep him busy and out of my beeswax for awhile.*

I grabbed my snuggle-muffins, aka Booboo, and Khronos, scootched under the covers, and fell asleep with a smile on my face, despite all the bad in the world.

Just one day of happiness . . . would I get my wish?

I awoke to a gentle nudge, squinting up to see Curjan standing over me. I bolted upright. "What's going on? Is something happening?"

He shook his head. "No, everything's fine, Princess. Your mother and father sent me to wake you; we're about to have Christmas breakfast, and she said her cinnamon rolls are your favorite."

"Cinnamon rolls! I'm in!" I screeched, jumping out of bed, forgetting about my Christmas jammies with the puppies and kittens plastered all over them.

He smirked as he eyed them quizzically, but said nothing, popping back out of the room and giving me space to get dressed.

I grumbled. "Well, don't show up in a girl's room if you don't wanna' see something that might be better left unseen." I figured my jammies were probably only the start of my morning issues, adding stank breath, eye boogers, and bedhead to the list of things I'd rather Curjan not get an eyeful of. I obviously had to talk to Mom about sending in one of the women next time she wanted to wake me. *Awkward.*

I jumped into the shower and got ready as fast as I could,

not wanting to look like a greaseball in the plethora of Christmas pics I knew my mother would insist on taking. Satisfied with my entry into the "Ugliest Christmas Sweater" contest—a poorly hand-embroidered Grinch holding an "I'm on the Naughty List" sign, thank you very much—and the wave of my almost-auburn locks and minimal makeup, I flashed to the kitchen, where the revelry was already in full swing.

"Dudes, you started without me?" I complained, jumping on the half-eaten tray of cinnamon buns.

"You snooze, you lose, Bay," shouted Matt with his mouth full, obviously high on icing already.

"Har har, how original, Matty," I snarked, dishing myself out two rolls with extra icing, and turning down the fruit salad passed my way. "I can't have any healthy flavors interfering with this extreme level of deliciousness," I offered Tara by way of explanation for my fruit snobbery.

I dug in, pouring myself some coffee to cleanse the palate between heavenly bites. Dad and Charlie were laughing at how seriously I took the rolls—*don't mess with my Yuletide traditions, man*—especially not with this many people partaking. I had to protect what was mine.

After breakfast was cleaned up and put away, we built a fire in the living room fireplace, and I reveled in the Christmas energy; it was cozy, warm, and full of laughter and the people I loved. The dogs and bravest of the cats mingled with our guests, and we commenced our gift exchange, where I was stoked to see that most of Charlie's clan had chosen to give each other gag gifts instead of something serious.

Tara had gotten Bradley his very own copy of the "Vegan Cupcakes Take Over the World" cookbook, which got a laugh but also my hearty approval. Matt got his brother Jake a pink kitty flea collar, *(get it, because they're cats in their shifter form),* and Jake bartered it for Ruth's Axe body wash, touting its "manly scent" as a perfect reason for the exchange.

Charlie had drawn my name, and I unwrapped some awesome black jeans and thermal Underarmour, courtesy of the emo shop in the mall, which would perfectly enhance my ninja wardrobe and yet was also very thoughtful. I gave him a hug. "Thank you, Uncle Charlie," I whispered in his ear. "Don't tell anyone this, but I kinda love you."

He smiled back. "I kinda love you too, Miss Baylee Girl. It will be our little secret."

I got the warm fuzzies. He really was the perfect uncle, and I wanted to savor the relationship we were building.

I was the recipient of a ton of gifts which the others didn't have, Mom apologizing and explaining that she'd already bought most of them before they'd shown up last week. Everyone settled down to watch me open my pile, and the attentiveness was both sweet and embarrassing at the same time.

No vibe-crashing on Christmas, Bay, I reminded myself, digging in. I didn't plan on anything dampening my enthusiasm for my solo gift opening party, an enthusiasm which had never waned despite the ever-advancing age which left me tottering on the precipice of adulthood.

I was most curious to see if Dad had actually bought me anything, at least anything that Mom didn't tell him to . . .

I ripped through the gifts, thanking my parents as I went, and piling up the new clothes to try on later. My mom had a decent sense of what I liked, so I typically didn't return many of the outfits she bought me. Since Mom and I were on a budget, Christmas tended to account for a big chunk of my winter wardrobe; no complaints here.

Better than showing up at school—or a war—looking like an urchin, I wryly though to myself.

I really didn't see anything I thought was all Dad, which was disappointing, until I got to the last gift—a small, non-descript box shoved way back under the tree so far I'd almost missed it. Matt fished it out and handed it to me, and suddenly Dad showed a lot more interest in my activities.

Huh, could it be . . .

I unhesitantly ripped into it, and inside there was just a single piece of folded-up paper. I reached for it, and Dad leaned forward, holding his breath.

It was a note from him, and scrawled on it was a single sentence: "This entitles the bearer of this IOU, Baylee Valec, to a new car of her choice—within reason—and is valid any time within the next year. Love, Dad."

I fell over, shocked. "Dad!" I shrieked, jumping up and into his arms. "This is so incredible! Thank you! I know my little Saturn will miss me, but I can always bequeath her to Matt," I stuck my tongue at out him. "When can we go look, huh, huh?" I was beyond excited, and he was beyond pleased with my reaction.

He twirled me about the room while Mom looked on, a big smile lighting her face. "Well, I never got to spoil you these past 18 years, so I'll pour it all into one year and buy you the car of your dreams. We might need to hold off, though, until we take care of our little issues. We don't want a war destroying your first new car, now do we?"

I reluctantly shook my head. "No, I guess not. Ugh. Fine,

fine, I hear ya," I grumbled, and then perked up. "But this gives me incentive to take care of these losers real quick-like, so I can get my new wheels and show them off around town." I beamed at everyone in the room. "I may even let you all take a ride with me, if you're lucky. In fact, if you're good to me, I shall bestow each of you with that honor." I faked using my queenly wand and granting them each my favor.

Curjan snorted. "I'm not sure if that's an honor or a punishment, Princess. I'll reserve judgment on that until I actually see your driving."

I pooh poohed him, and then Dad quieted us all. He then got down on one knee and proposed—for the second time—to the woman of his dreams.

Of course Mom, aka Candice Valec, soon to be Candice Essene, accepted with a big, gross smooch, and then showed off a rock that was even bigger than the first one she'd sported. I relented and gave them a public hug and kiss, throwing up a little at the newfound sweetness of my parental family unit.

We settled in as an extended family and argued over what to binge watch, finally settling for a Wolverine movie marathon, ending later that night with "Logan" and not a dry eye in the house.

The day was as perfect as any I'd ever had, and I never wanted it to end. But, like all good things, end it did.

As I crawled into bed that night, I couldn't help but wonder what tomorrow would bring. Something told me it wasn't going to be good.

Chapter 23: Ransacking Goes Both Ways

I was up at the crack of whatever comes after dawn, sleepy and yawning my way into the kitchen for some coffee and hopefully a leftover cinnamon roll. I ran into Charlie and Dad having a serious conversation in the corner of the room, and they motioned me over to join them.

"So, Bay, we've been thinking about that note that was stuck in the hole where you fished out the camera in New York. We're wondering if 'watch video' could be referring to the setup in the bunker near your house that I was unwittingly guarding. It's time for us to get proactive with finding this second key; we need to take a team down there to see if that's the case. Thoughts?" I was tickled Dad was actually considering my opinion. *Progress.*

"It's totally worth a shot, given that we don't have much else to go on right now anyway. I'm in." I was tired of hiding out and ready for some action.

We gathered a team of all but two of our people, Rebecca and Tara, who would stay behind to guard Mom and the hideout. They'd let us know if there were any problems and we could immediately flash back if needed. We decided to split up, six flashing directly inside the bunker, and five who would pop into our house to make sure all was well there.

I was on Team Bunker with Curjan, Daniel, Charlie, Jake, and Curtis, while the others went with Dad to the house. I missed my room and wanted to pick up a few things, but if it was safe I could always stop by afterward and grab some stuff for me and my critter family.

Cur and Daniel made great generals, coaching us before we left on how to land with our backs to one another in preparation to defend against anything already present in the small space. My nerves were on edge, but I steeled my spine and flashed on "Go" with the rest of them.

I felt a sense of achievement when I landed exactly as practiced, my back in line with the others as we circled the wagons for safety. Luckily, the place was empty and dark, and appeared as though it hadn't been touched since we nabbed the key last week.

The very fact that no one had been here was odd enough to me . . . one would think that it would be torn apart once they realized the key was missing. I didn't have a good understanding of how these nasty ninjas thought and operated, so I made a mental note to ask the others about it at our next family meeting.

Curtis and Jake rushed to the computer equipment while the rest of us stood guard and looked around the rest of the room for any clues or cameras. There wasn't much to unearth in the tiny space, and I avoided all reminders of my bonding time with the port-a-john, still standing like an eerie sentinel in the corner. Suddenly Curtis and Jake high-fived, grabbed up the hard drives they'd disconnected from the monitors, and motioned for us to flash to my house, where we could talk more freely.

We arrived to chaos, as Dad, Bradley, Matt, Ruth, and Smith milled about, aimlessly picking up and discarding broken chunks of our television set, our refrigerator, destroyed knick knacks and pictures . . . our whole life, reduced to shards.

I was floored and confused, and struggled to understand what my eyes and mind were telling me.

"Dad, what's going on?" I cried.

He flashed to my side, cradling my head against his chest. "Baylee, honey, I'm so sorry. It looks like Phoebus' goons were here, probably looking for the key. They've tossed the place, and pretty much ensured they destroyed everything in their path in the process. There's not much that isn't broken, I'm afraid." He ran his hands through his hair, worry and stress lining his face.

"Mom's gonna doody number twody herself about this," I fretted, looking around the room. "How bad are the bedrooms . . . and our precious cat room?"

Charlie walked over. "I'm sorry, too, sweet child. While I can't say it's unexpected, it's still devastating. I'm so glad no one was here when those ignorant imbeciles showed up. This is what I was afraid of. Come, let's go upstairs and have a look around, shall we? I'll be with you every step of the way."

I'd gone numb. I stumbled my way upstairs, not even bothering to flash, needing the connection to the earth I got from planting my foot on each step and pulling myself up by the handrail. Even our gates at the top and bottom of the stairway separating the cats from dogs were destroyed, and the emotional pain was enough to yank me from my dazed state.

"How DARE they!" I vented, not even bothering to keep my voice down. "They destroyed even my pets' things? These precious creatures never lifted a tooth to harm any of these flippin' yahoos, and they have the balls to come into MY home and destroy the meager possessions of my animal family?"

I raced up the stairs now, propelled by rage and righteous anger. The cat room was equally annihilated, all the many weekends and evenings of work Mom and I had put into their safe haven destroyed in a single hour. And for what? Simple cruelty's sake?

There was no other explanation.

It was, ironically, at that moment that I truly faced the depth of the menacing evil we were up against. I thought I'd understood just how disgusting these folks were when I'd seen and heard what they'd done to Dad, Merle, Krupert, Curjan, and Samantha. Now that they'd ruthlessly destroyed everything Mom and I had built with our bare hands, the items we'd lovingly chosen to complete our little haven, the sacrifices we'd made to ensure that everyone was safe and happy, I finally got it.

They were evil.

And evil must be banished.

My worldview had turned to black and white. With maybe just a touch of red, for the burning rage that had ignited in my soul.

I grabbed some clothes that hadn't been ruined for Mom

and me, as well as some of the cat and dog toys I salvaged from the wreckage. I looked around in disgust. I didn't know when I'd be able to come back here, but I was hiring someone to put it back together before I did, so I wouldn't have to be retraumatized by the damage they'd inflicted. It was just too painful. I never knew how attached I'd become to my home until my sense of safety was violated from within its four walls.

I was also getting a better sense of my attachment to Mom and the life we'd built together. No, it hadn't been perfect, and, like any teenager, I'd filed my share of grievances against her, but now that everything we had was gone, I missed it with every fiber of my being.

Even my bed was shredded. I sat gingerly on its edge, shoulders heaving with loss and misery. Charlie popped out to grab me some tissues, and Curjan came back in behind him, going down on his knees to look into my tear-filled eyes.

"We'll get the bastards who did this, Princess." He gently wiped the tracks from my cheeks. His face hardened, and he looked truly menacing in that moment. "I won't rest until we do."

He stood, grabbed me by the hand, and flashed us both back to the house by the river.

I didn't even get to say goodbye.

Chapter 24: Video Evidence

Everyone was crowded into the living room, eyes on the flat screen TV, as Curtis and Jake worked to project what they were finding on the hard drives so we could all see it. There were years of raw footage from every single place the members of Dad's elite warriors were chained. How could we possibly sort through all that?

Jake believed that the footage we were meant to see, if it was indeed here, would be from the past six months. Therefore we broke into teams of two to run through month-long segments from the New York junkyard where Curjan and Samantha had been chained.

We could save the rest of the footage—of Dad's other warriors in dog form—for later to try to figure out where they were, but for now we needed to focus on finding this second key and moving it to safety. Matt asked if I'd like to work together, and I reluctantly agreed, not wanting to set off another territorial dispute between Curjan and Matt.

I'm no one's property, I reminded myself, awed that I even had to give myself a reminder of such a thing.

Matt and I took the footage Jake offered and headed downstairs to cue it up on the entertainment center. Others broke off into twos and borrowed laptops or other devices to view the footage. We decided to grab some sodas and chips to munch on while we watched, and I was sorry I did when I witnessed the footage of Curjan suffering starvation and thirst at the end of his chain. I pushed the bowl away, sickened to my core, as I saw the man I couldn't deny a connection to writhe in agony.

Our footage was from the middle of summer, and the heat must have been extreme. Curjan paced, his skeletal body heaving beneath the shaggy, matted coat. He raised his nose to the air, scenting for food and water, but lowered it again, disappointment showing starkly in his eyes. He fell to the ground, seemingly suffering heatstroke—which would kill a normal dog—yet due to his immortality, he repeatedly and wearily came "back to life" within moments.

He tried to comfort Samantha, who didn't even bother to pace or walk, but lay on the ground nearby, a skeletal bump on an otherwise pock-marked landscape. My heart was again rent in two as I was forced to scroll through not minutes, not hours, but days of their pitiful existences, to fully comprehend the depths of the depravity of their captors, and the bitterness hardened into a gnarled knot in my gut.

Matt was similarly-affected, although he was better at hiding it than I was. He cleared his throat. "Wow, this isn't easy to watch, eh?"

My head drooped. "I can't believe I went from the most wonderful Christmas of my life just yesterday to the destruction of so much I hold dear and a bird's eye view of the utter soullessness of our enemies today. I confess that I'm feeling helpless to do what needs to be done in the face of such evil." I grabbed his arm. "I might need a pep talk, Matty."

He swept me into a one-armed hug. "Free pep talk, coming right up. But first, let's pop back upstairs and see if anyone else found anything. Maybe some good news will cheer us up."

The others had much the same idea we'd had, converging again on the living room and flopping on couches and chairs, filling in on the rugs as space permitted. A heavy silence ensued. Charlie raised his hand to take the floor. "Please report in ONLY if you found anything in your footage. We can process what we were forced to watch later, but for now let's see if there's any good news in this ugly day. Anyone?"

Bradley and Smith raised their hands. "We did, sir. We thought you'd want to take a look at this. Curtis, can you cue up that footage we mentioned?"

Curtis simply nodded and had it all set up within minutes.

On the screen, we witnessed all the similarities to what we'd just viewed downstairs, although I could tell from the date stamp it was from just a few days ago . . . the day we'd found Curjan! The excitement in the room grew.

First we watched as Curjan jumped one of the ninjas who came into the camera area, efficiently ripping out his throat in much the same way he'd ripped out the throat of the man who'd threatened me. I was heartsick all over again, but struggled to maintain my dignity. *Keep it together, Bay.*

Then he and Samantha lured the other man into the area between the two of them and ensnared him with their chains, she wrapping hers around his feet and Cur quickly encircling his neck.

The man struggling but was trapped and became bound to them through their tethers, much like a member of their pack. It appeared they were then able to instruct him through the bond to free them from their mind-control collars and thus their chains. He fought their domination briefly, but in the end followed through with their release. Ingenious!

Curjan spoke up then. "Don't get too excited about our plan, or our general level of competence; we got lucky with the tether binding him mentally to us, because we had no idea that would happen. Our sole goal had been to imprison him with our chains and try to force him to free us. I don't believe it would have worked if the tethers hadn't been acting as mindlinks." His grim expression belied the angst he felt at having to witness the brutality, both his own as well as that of his captors. I felt for him on so many levels.

Soon both dogs were freed by their captive, at which point Cur dispatched him too, and then the alarm sounded and the two dogs ran for the exit. The camera footage was blank for awhile after that, so we fast-forwarded to an hour later, when three men entered the enclosure, dug up the same small trunk we'd found, and removed a glass case, which we could only assume held the second key.

As the men turned, we got a good look at their uniforms, noticing for the first time that they were not wearing the standard black ninja attire we'd seen on most of our attackers. Instead, these men where wearing maintenance uniforms—dark gray in color with black name and company patches.

There, in big bold letters across the left-side pocket, were four letters. MoMA.

Mom jumped up and whipped out some in-your-face gloating, shouting, "I told you it was the Museum of Modern Art! That's where they took the key! They've got people on the inside there, and dollars to donuts it's being hidden somewhere in that museum."

We looked at each others, slack-jawed with amazement. *Damn if the Mominator wasn't smarter than the whole lot of us.*

I guess I know where we're going now. And I didn't think we were leaving Mom behind this time.

CHAPTER 25: NYC, Take Two

After a short logistical meeting—during which Dad and Charlie reassured us that the first key was safe in Perrin—we all packed our stuff to head out. We expected to be gone overnight, but since one could never say for sure, we planned accordingly. Dad brought down more of his most-trusted Perrinite guards to watch over the house and our precious animal friends, while we made secret plans through grouplink as to who was entrusted with keeping Mom safe: EVERYONE.

It was well-understood that she was the most vulnerable amongst us, not only because she was solely human, but also because if they succeeded in kidnapping her they'd have power over both the king and myself. Dad and I would do anything to for my mom, and the bad guys would know that, or at least presume it to be true. Every member of the team had to be extra vigilant to ensure her safety at all times.

We repeated a similar protocol to our first trip: flashing to the Baltimore train station and then traveling by rail to Philly, where we flashed directly to the same hotel chain but a different location, just in case the first had been compromised. Mom held up well to a trip of that length, and I was impressed by her stalwartness—another two-dollar vocab builder I'd memorized in English class this year, and I was oddly pleased with myself for finding a way to use it in a sentence. *Dork.*

A mere four hours start to finish, and we were tucked into our double suite. Bradley's mindchime, aka "the cone of silence", was in full effect as we planned to storm the castle, aka the Museum of Modern Art. The last thing we needed was to be overheard by anyone, especially the evil ninjas, about a conspiracy to break into such a high-profile target.

That would not go over well in any scenario.

Mom assured us that the museum would be well-protected through the use of state-of-the-art alarm systems, cameras, and 24/7 security staff, making it difficult for us to just stroll in and explore at will. The website for MoMA boasted of a revolving collection of 200,000 pieces, and I for one was ready to give up before we even started. How could we possibly find a key—probably in the shape of a chess piece if the first was anything to go by—in a place of that size?

We decided the only intelligent thing to do was to take a tour of the place, yet that plan in and of itself was not without a long list of problems. If we were spotted on camera, and we would be, how could we keep our identities secret when the Nefarious Ninjas knew what so many of us looked like? Not only that, but their cameras would have caught the group of us on film at the junkyard, and so everyone who'd been there would be readily recognized if the footage was monitored.

We had to assume we were all known to them, since they knew we captured the first key and had found their second hiding place along with Cur, too.

Dilemmas.

THE CURSE OF CUR

Mom wanted to go it alone, but that idea was instantly kiboshed by Dad, Charlie, me, and, well, everyone really. *Just NO.*

As we approached late afternoon and time was running out, we made a snap decision to send in Bradley and Tara, since they were the least likely to be on Phoebus radar. The two often stayed behind to guard Mom and the property, and were also our two quietest team members, tending to stay in the background when crappola was hitting the fan.

Matt flashed out and procured two wigs—a curly blond fro for Bradley, which cracked everyone up, and a black vixen wig for Tara, which only made her look hot in a whole new way. Charlie's eyes sparked with laughter when she tried it on, but I also caught a shred of, what was that, interest? *Mrawhr!*

Charlie gave me the evil eye, and I grinned, loving that I'd gotten under his skin.

"You know you're my favorite uncle, Charlie," I quipped through our mindlink. "And if you're not gay, then you have to endure all my best heterosexual innuendos from here on out. You can't get off that easily!" I flashed him an innocent smile, with just a dose of mwahaha toward the end.

"Just remember, then, it's tit for tat, young lady—and I have plenty of material to work with between Cur and Matt," he rejoined, making a kissy face at me while he one-upped me yet again.

Snort. Charlie said tit. *And, ah hell, he's right. He does have the goods on me . . . dognabbit.* My joy deflated in the face of such undeniable mastery.

Tara and Bradley popped themselves a block away from the museum and kept in contact with the group through the king's tether as they worked. They slipped inside through the front visitor entrance like any other tourist, keeping up a running commentary about the pieces they were seeing and any possible hiding places the art could be concealing.

Unfortunately, the size of the place was as daunting as we'd all expected, but we decided we had no choice but to flash inside in the middle of the night and check things out for ourselves. No one was interested in setting off those all too active alarms and ending up in the clanker. Especially since most of the team didn't exist in any databases on Earth . . . that would indeed make for some odd lines of questioning.

Bradley and Tara stayed until they were forced out at 5:30, and had only gotten through about 1/3 of the rooms by then. They had, though, by virtue of deductive reasoning, postulated that the object was most-likely hidden in the permanent collection rooms as opposed to the temporary installations, on the off-chance it could be moved without their knowledge.

A lively discussion ensued about possible hiding places, and with the MoMA staff compromised we had a lot less to go on than we'd hoped. There was no way we could trust anyone there to question them.

Nonetheless, despite these feelings of hopelessness, we grabbed ourselves some more of that delicious pizza and hit the hay, opting for a few hours of shuteye before Operation MoMA Stealthfest kicked into high gear.

I thought I wouldn't be able to sleep due to all the anxiety, but I was out like a light, and only woke to Matt shaking me at 2:30. "Bay, wakey wakey. Everyone's up, and it's your turn in the bathroom. Make it quick, we want to flash out of here exactly at 3:00."

I threw my pillow at him, grumbling as I stumbled my way to the bathroom. Truth be told, it kinda stunk to have to contain my morning grumpiness around these people . . . I enjoyed being a beeyotch when I first got up, with no one but Mom and the critters around to bear witness to me at my worst.

Sue me: not a morning person, emkay?

Now I had to be on better behavior even when I had no desire to be, and as most teenagers would affirm, I wasn't accustomed to dialing it down. *Ugh. Adulting sucks.*

I decided to jump in the shower to wake myself up, but forewent washing my hair since it took too long to dry. I needed to be on my game, and for that I had to be awake. Thank Dog there was copious amounts of coffee waiting for me when I strolled out of the bathroom, and I didn't feel quite so bad when I realized everyone else was in varying stages of grumpypants as well.

Bradley again surrounded us with the mindchime to protect us from wandering ears, and Curjan started. "I've run many missions like this in my time as part of the king's guard, so today I've asked to take lead. We can't possibly cover this entire museum in one night, BUT we will start at the permanent collection site and hope we get lucky. That's on the 5th floor. We'll flash directly there, and then split up in teams of two, moving out to search each room. Remember, though, that the walls are all hot, as are most of the art pieces. If you touch them, there's a good chance an alarm will go off, and then our cover is blown." He placed me with him, which immediately caused awkwardidity for both Matt and me.

Aw, hells. I thought to myself. *I'd probably get butthurt whether he put me on his team or not, just because. Bah. Men.*

Curjan, and the world, continued on while I wallowed. "Jake and Curtis will flash immediately to the security room and put the guards in a mindbind, giving us about two hours before they wake up again in time for shift change. Then they will monitor the cameras and comms, letting us know if there are any developments that require us to remove ourselves immediately from the vicinity. We've got to be out of there before 5:30. Am I clear?" Heads nodded.

He looked directly at me. "Most importantly, don't touch anything, unless and until you are SURE it has Perrinite written all over it. Keep in touch through the mindlinks, and may we find what we're searching for. Good luck, warriors."

We moved out, landing directly into the largest room on the 5th floor. Curjan motioned toward areas he wanted the teams to search, and motioned for me to follow him. I tried my best to use the ninja stealth he'd been teaching me, but I still looked and felt like a clumsy oaf traipsing along behind him. I was deputy-dog nervous about breaking and entering—well, at least the illegality of the entering part—and I wasn't interested in getting my first felony at the tender age of 17.

I didn't know what room we were in, but he motioned for me to search the left side while he focused on the right. I ignored the wall artwork to the best of my ability, although I'd never been in this fancy of an art gallery and was semi-curious if there were pieces here I'd actually recognize from either my art classes or Mom's ramblings. I figured it would be harder for them to hide the key under or in a painting, which left the sculptures of more interest to the amateur detective eye I was attempting to emulate.

Curjan had told us that both he and Daniel, the two defacto war generals who worked directly under the King and Charlie, could detect Perrinite "vibes" as opposed to those left by most earthlings. Anyone who saw anything out of the ordinary was to call one or both of the men to check suspicious objects before removal.

Dad jumped into the mindlink, calling for Curjan, a sense of urgency in his voice. We flashed three rooms down, where everyone had congregated around an odd statue with a plate listing the artist as Joan Miro, 1936. I had no idea what it meant or symbolized, but Mom said it was one of her favorites, and featured a stuffed parrot on a wooden perch. The bird sat overtop a pair of stuffed pantyhose dangling in a wooden cutout frame, with a black derby hat and an old-fashioned map tacked onto the front.

Um . . . way to take a bunch of crap, throw it together, and call it art, there, Joan Miro. Geesh! If I did that in my school, I'd be laughed out the door, but this guy's junk's sitting in the middle of the Museum of Modern Art. I shook my head.

Mom whispered. "What kind of animal does Phoebus turn into, honey?"

A light went off in Dad's head. "Aw, you might be onto something, my sweet. I can see it was a good move bringing you with us! Phoebus turns into a bird . . . he and his whole clan can choose what bird they'd like to represent, but you're right, he might hide it somewhere that he found funny or symbolic. Well done!" He grinned enthusiastically, like she'd just won a Nobel Prize or something.

Turning to Cur, he asked, "Do you detect any Perrinite vibratory signatures from it?" Cur and Daniel both concentrated, then nodded—we'd found it!

We called Jake and Curtis in from security, and they took pics of the map on the front of the sculpture—just in case it meant anything—and then dad took the plunge, thrusting his hand inside the sculpture and coming out with a similar glass box, only smaller, than the one we'd found in the bunker in Culpeper.

This time, though, the key was green and cut into the shape of the knight, which to the layman's eye would have appeared as just another piece of the sculpture. *Well played, Phoebus, ya psycho.*

We were shocked by a sudden blare of alarms—even though we should have expected it—and even moreso by the harsh voice that came over the loudspeaker: "Enjoy your second key, Randulf. We're recreating those two as we speak, so your copies will be useless anyway. You're on a fool's mission; you'll never be able to stop our divine plan to rid ourselves of the plague engulfing both Perrin and Earth.

"Have a nice day. Oh, and I'll see you REAL soon, Baylee."

We looked at each other, eyes wide, and then flashed as planned to a second hotel, in case the first had been compromised.

That was bat guano-scary close.

Too close—and our getaway too easy, given that Phoebus knew we were there all along. It seemed our efforts were all for naught . . . we were being toyed with by an smirking evil far greater than I'd ever dreamed possible.

Now. What.

CHAPTER 26: YEAH, NOW WHAT?

D isheartened and freaked out. That's what we were. Well, I was, at least.

The room was quiet, with the exception of the stress-filled breathing of my compatriots, who awkwardly milled about and tried to avoid bumping into each other in the crowded hotel room.

Shoulda got a suite.

I spoke up, working through our situation out loud, more for my benefit than anyone else's. "So, let's see if I have this straight: Bad guy, aka Phoebus, fathers a kid with a human hundreds of years ago. This was a no-no, and triggers a prophecy about the destruction of Earth and Perrin at the hands of this bloodline. Perrinites are then forbidden to journey to earth in hopes the tainted gene pool will die out on its own. A curse is set up on those who defy the order, the effects of which used to be secret, but we now know turns them to their animal counterpart—except they remain in a feral, or wild, state. They never remember being anything other than an animal, and effectively spend eternity as any earth-bound critter would."

Everyone listened raptly, despite the fact that they knew all this already. "Then 20 years ago, the Prophetess Shanti sees another vision confirming that The Scion has been born on Earth. The predicted devastation to both Perrin and Earth is even worse than the first vision, and, unbeknownst to us, sets in motion Phoebus' recruitment of a pack of ne'er-do-well ninja types and they begin plans—and take action—to bring the prophecy to fruition. Do I have it so far?"

Curjan looked sad. "Yes, Princess, that's pretty much it in a nutshell."

I continued, pacing as much as I could in the crowded space. "Then, a year later, Shanti has another vision, that of a similar birth between an Earthling and a Perrinite, which gives hope to Perrin that The Scion can be conquered and our worlds saved. As a result, my father comes to Earth to sacrifice himself by creating the anti-scion, knowing that he will be struck feral after doing so. What he doesn't realize is that his whole team will end up wild too as a result of his exceptionally strong mindlink with them."

Dad hung his head, overwhelmed with guilt and grief. I kept going though, warming up to my synopsis now. "He finds Mom, is struck by the god of love, and yadda yadda yadda, here I am. The supposed anti-scion, aka The Redeemer. Or, as I like to call it, toast." That got a few laughs.

I was struck by a thought. "Dad, whose voice was that on the loudspeaker at the museum?"

"Phoebus, honey. That was Phoebus."

"Ugh. So that bastage spends the past 20 years building a mind-control tether capable of enslaving everyone on Perrin and Earth, tests it out on you and your team, and then spreads you around the country guarding keys to this finally-perfected Minion Machine. What I don't understand is, if these keys are so easy to replicate, what would be the point of hiding them? If he was discovered by the government before he was ready to take over our worlds, couldn't the government then just as easily create their own duplicate keys?"

"Good point, Baylee," replied Charlie, rubbing his chin. He loved a puzzle. "King, we need to quickly get this second key up to Perrin for analysis to see if there's anything about these chesspiece-style keys that would make them impossible to replicate. There's the very real chance that he's lying to us—that he wasn't yet prepared for a fight, and that we got to the first two keys before he realized we were figuring things out. We've now lost that element of surprise, which will make the remaining three pieces incredibly difficult to obtain."

Great, this was all about to get even harder? *Curse my monkey-in-the-jungle life.*

Feeling a little less downtrodden now that there was hope we hadn't spent all this search-time in vain, we hopped the next airwaves to the Philly Train station and retraced our steps through Baltimore, taking care to ensure we weren't followed.

The last thing I wanted was another ninja brawl right now . . . my bed and critters were calling to me. Let Dad and Charlie deal with getting the second key safely to Perrin and on its way to analysis. I was throwing on my Christmas jammies and crawling into bed with BooBoo, Una, and Khronos.

A smile lit my face when I saw that our woodland hideaway was still intact and all was well. I would fall asleep to the sound of Christmas music through my headphones, warm and snuggled with my favorite beings and a mound of blankets. For one moment, I could pretend our world was indeed a happy place.

It may be one of the last moments I'll get.

Chapter 27: Those Durn Keys

My first thoughts upon awakening weren't sugarplums, or even boys, but *did they analyze those ever-lovin' keys yet?*

The wheels were already spinning, and to my mind, our whole quest depended on the answer to that question. Are these keys able to be duplicated, or was Phoebus trying to throw us off the track?

I still didn't want to get out of bed, though, even with all the excessive brain swarming. I was snuggled with my best buddies, and I reminded myself this was supposed to be my Christmas break from school. Normally I'd be in total slug wallow mode—sleeping until noon, playing video games, and going to the mall and movies with Amaya. *You know, normal teen crappola.*

Instead, here was yours truly, caught up in stuff I had no business being caught up in. I wanted to be angry at my father for dragging Mom and I into this mess, but that was a luxury I couldn't bankroll at the moment. I promised myself that when this was all over—assuming I was still in one piece—I'd indulge in the biggest teen fit ever known to Perrin-kind. I fantasized about the conniption I'd throw; I'd yell and scream, maybe throw a few things, and definitely tell let a few "I hate you's" rip.

For now, I'd have to put on my big girl panties and save the world.

But after that? A daughter's revenge! *Mwahaha.*

Uh oh. Maybe my car should come before fit throwing—but THEN—yeah, revenge.

Dad called a meeting through the mindlink (this was turning out to be super handy), and I popped out of bed, hoping for some good news for once.

We rendezvoused in the training room, because this was serious biz now, and Dad held up his hand for quiet. "Our experts on Perrin worked through the night to analyze the keys for us. If you remember, the first, in the shape of a chess king, is black, and we now have confirmation it was created from the most precious stone in both dimensions: megtenate. Has anyone heard of it?" We all shook our heads.

"It's similar to black diamond, only even harder, and doesn't exist on the Earth plane, at least not to anyone's knowledge. The second is a deep green, and is hewn into the shape of a chess knight. It's a stone also known for its diamond-like strength, called emaranite. This Perrinite stone is extremely rare, and has only been obtained in small quantities from the depths of the ocean."

Everyone waited breathlessly for the rest . . . I was too impatient. "And, Dad? Can they be easily duplicated?"

The King managed to look both indulgent and irritated with me at once, a trait which I myself would like to perfect. "Our experts say no. These stones, and the cut, should make it fairly difficult. The best news of all is something that Krupert has remembered from studying them. He believes that they created these one-of-a-kind chesspieces *first*, and *then* poured the metal over them to cast the key slots, specifically so they couldn't be copied. Which means that even if they were to chisel new ones, the chances of them not fitting the key slots have gone up exponentially. In a nutshell, belief on Perrin amongst the experts and intel we've gathered from those we've captured is that Phoebus lied to us—and he is moving the other keys as we speak."

A cheer went up around the room, and my knees almost gave out on me, my relief was so great. At least we weren't starting from scratch.

They were onto us now. There were things they knew that we wished they didn't—namely that we'd been able to bring those we'd rescued back from feral state and hence learned things they'd thought would remain secret—but now we'd have to move on from here and figure out how to get those other keys and rescue Dad's remaining warriors.

For now, we should celebrate.

Charlie seemed to know what I was thinking, and held up a hand to gain the floor. "Hold on, everyone. Before we get too excited about this news, we should take a moment to debate a very important question: should we just destroy the two keys in our possession, and set back their plans by years in doing so? Thoughts?"

Curjan shook his head. "I really don't think that's wise, Charlie. If they learn we've destroyed the keys and there's no hope in getting them back from us, what's to stop them from killing all our kidnapped warriors, as well as all the other Perrinites they've brainwashed? Not only that, but our scientists would probably like to study the machine before destruction so we can put a stop to something like this happening in the future. Yes, it would make it easier for right now, but it puts too many of our people in danger. That's my opinion. I, of course, defer to King Randulf for the final decision, but I know he and I both want our team safely removed from their clutches before taking any drastic steps."

Everyone reluctantly nodded his or her head in agreement. Most on Perrin had evolved to a point where they truly valued each and every life, and the people currently trapped in feral mindsets and guarding keys were a big part of Cur and Dad's lives. They couldn't just be thrown away.

My heart sank. I knew it was the right thing to do, but I was selfishly scared about what would come next, and how I was going to figure out where to go from here. I felt so much pressure that somehow this all rested on my shoulders, and I was too young to have this much responsibility.

Suddenly I felt an arm go around my shoulders, and I was pulled into Matt's warm embrace. "It's going to be OK, Baylee. I promise. What do you say we take a little bit of downtime for ourselves? I remember someone promising me a movie date in one of those fancy theatres with the recliners . . . wanna get out of here?"

I smiled. "Ho, yeah, you bet your manly buns I do! Ooh, let's go to my favorite Chinese restaurant first, too. And, best of all, we won't even need my old wheels to get us there!" I could feel my face flush with excitement.

Anything to distract me from the shize-storm that lay ahead.

I called out, "Mom, Dad! Matt and I are gonna pop over to Ashburn to the Hong Kong and then to the Dulles Regal. Before you ask, no, we don't need an entourage . . . after all, with us flashing it's not like they can follow us, right?"

Mom and Dad looked at each other, then at me, before

Mom reluctantly agreed. "OK, honey, but keep in touch with your father through the mind-thingy, please. Take one of the burner phones with you, just in case, and make sure you're back before dark. You should be able to eat early and hit a matinee, so you're home safe and sound by 5:00. Deal?" She came over and squeezed the life out of me.

"Ugh, Mother, fi-ennnn! Now, get off'a me. I gotta go get ready!" I squealed. As I flashed to my room and then the closest bathroom to shower and make myself pretty, I pretended not to see the storm clouds gathering over Curjan's head, or the frown on his handsome face.

Bite me, Sexy. Nothing is getting in the way of this much-needed downtime. Not even the brooding but gorgeous man some idiot (i.e. the voice in my head) claims is my mate. Not in this lifetime.

Chapter 28: Second Dates

I was all smiles by the time I'd showered and dressed in my new slinky top—courtesy of Amaya—combined with the new skinny jeans Mom had bought me for Christmas. Glancing in the mirror, I was surprised that I actually felt pretty good about the girl looking back at me, a new experience to be sure.

Mom was always jelly belly about my height, said at 5'8" I could pull off just about any outfit; she often teased me that she'd make me her personal dress up doll if I'd let her. Today my hazel eyes and auburn hair both shone, and my skin looked radiant too. *Maybe those Perrin genes are kickin' in*, I thought. I wasn't complaining.

I strolled on into the kitchen, where the crowd I thought of as my family was caught up in a rousing game of Uno. I couldn't help but laugh as they good-naturedly ribbed and demeaned each other, and then I looked up and caught Curjan's approving gaze.

He popped into my head via the mental tether, something he hadn't often done one on one. "You look beautiful, Princess. I'm concerned for your safety today, but I trust you and Matt can handle yourselves. Remember to stay in touch with your father via mindlink, and have fun." He smirked, turning back to the game.

Huh. *He almost seems happy for me, which kinda pisses me off. The buttmunch. Reverse psychology, and it's so working on me!*

Not to be left speechless (for long), I rather lamely rejoined, "Oh, I'll have fun. Don'tchu worry about that, Cur my friend. I can handle myself if any ninjas come my way." *Bah, tongue-tied much, Bay? And . . . were those famous last words?* I hoped not.

I stuffed down the hurt feelings and said goodbye to the group, and then I grabbed Matt by the hand and attempted my first tag-along flash.

It went better than expected; at least we made it to the right location, although we did end up in a pile of leaves off to the side of the shopping center next to the Hong Kong Restaurant. *Awkward!*

Matt picked us both up and laughed, giving me a high five. "Hey, for your first time, you did pretty well. You'll learn to pick out of the way places to land as you go along, so you're not showing up in the middle of the restaurant, in a pile of leaves, or in a watermelon cart." He grinned, and I couldn't help but chuckle at the memory.

Wiping down my pants and top, I stepped onto the sidewalk and pointed at the restaurant. "Well, we made it at least. They make a mean General Tso's fake chicken, so I already know what I'm having. Ooh, plus some veggie spring rolls! Can. Not. Wait."

"Let's just make it two then, so I can see what all the hubbub is about."

I'd forgotten how much I genuinely liked Matt, but having him all to myself during the meal reminded me. When we were with everyone else, discussion and tensions ruled due to our plight, and any romantic overtures were noticed and commented on by the peanut gallery. Not only that, but the whole weird "mate" thing between Curjan and I had thrown us all for a loop.

I liked Matt. I'd liked Matt before Cur, and I still liked him just as much when we managed to grab some alone time to explore our connection.

After he'd gobbled his first helping of General Tso's, Matt got up to place another order and I couldn't help but smile. Boy could eat! I looked at my plate, and still had 1/3 of mine left . . . but I was determined to chow it all down. My own appetite had kicked up exponentially since opening to my Perrin half, so I understood why a big guy like Matt would need double the food intake that I did.

While we waited, Matt tentatively took my hand, and I smirked.

"Feeling shy all of a sudden, Big Boy?"

"I just don't know where we stand," he admitted, sharing the insecurity I'd been sensing since Cur came into the picture. My heart was in danger of spewing green ooze, so I tried to clamp down on it without shutting myself off, which wasn't easy to do.

"I'm confused too, Matty," I rejoined, trying to be honest with both him and myself about how I was feeling. "The jolt that went through me when I first saw Cur on that chain was like nothing I'd ever felt before or since. It was enough to knock me out . . . well, I guess that part was technically my heart chakra exploding open.

"But I'm not even 18 yet—not officially an adult on the Earth plane. The last thing I need to think about is a life partner; especially now, when I don't even know if I'll have a life to come back to when all is said and done. I don't need to get tied down to anyone, Earth boy or Perrin stud, but I still feel just as attracted to you as I ever did.

"I just think that attraction now comes with complications, err, baggage if you will. As to where that leaves us? I think if we like each other enough to see where it goes without strings or pressure, then that's what we should do. What do you think?"

I peeked up at him through my lashes. Now I was the one feeling shy, after expressing my true feelings, throwing the line out there. *Will I be rejected? Gulp. Monster-level terrifying!*

A wide smile pulled at his face, and he squeezed my hand. "That's all I'm asking for. I know you're young, I know there are complications besides the end of two worlds—but I like you, Baylee. I like you a LOT. If I'm being honest, more than I can remember liking anyone in a long, long time—I mean, we're talking decades here."

"Old man," I teased, but my heart was pounding out of my chest.

"Hot young thang," he teased back, leaning into me, and I looked up and into his eyes. I wasn't prepared for the intensity I saw in those deep chocolate irises, and I was done for—as his eyes burned into mine, his lips came down, lightly touching mine in a continuation of the tease, offering a promise of more to come.

"Um, here's your General Tso's, sir," the flustered counter girl said, dropping the tray like a hot potato and scurrying away.

We snickered together like a couple of love-struck teens,

Matt nuzzling me along the side of my cheek. *Uh oh*, my mind thought while my heart blissed out. *I think I'm in deep, deep doody.*

CHAPTER 29: THE MOVE
AT THE MOVIES

We agreed to see the latest super-hero movie, as I was secretly hoping I could learn some new moves while we were at it. *Fighting moves, Bay, fighting moves; get your mind out of the gutter.* Plus, come on, they're just fun to watch … and inspiring, especially now. I'd always loved super-heroes, and Robert Downey Jr.'s take on Ironman happened to be high on my list, mostly due to his snark factor. I mean, Mom drooled over him, but he was too dad for me.

Speaking of non-dads, Chris Hemsworth's Thor was never to be sneezed at, and Amaya and I could dish about him for hours, but that was for other, eh-hem, albeit very important reasons.

We lucked into an early showing of an Avengers flick, and I settled into the recliner next to Matt. I cradled a large bucket of popcorn and a soda—crucial necessities—and I begrudgingly agreed to share both with my handsome date, reminding him that when he scarfed them down he had to be the one to go get the free refills.

Date! I couldn't believe it. I hadn't been on a "real" date, if you didn't count our pizza outing, since my disastrous—and short-lived—romance with Rick last year.

Ugh, don't think about that cheater . . .

I pushed the old news out of my mind and settled in for a little slice of Bay heaven. Dark theatre (check). Incredibly handsome date (check). Movie accoutrements (check). Reclining chair in the back row (check). Long sweater to double as a blanket in case I got cold (check).

And . . . let the ultimate in escapism begin.

As the opening credits rolled, Matt leaned my way and I leaned his. He took hold of my hand under my blanket sweater and whispered in my ear. "Thank you for coming out with me today, Baylee. This is the happiest I've felt in, well, forever."

Charmed, I turned my head to brush my lips against his, returning the promise he'd offered earlier. He took the opportunity to deepen the kiss, and here in the darkened theatre, I opened myself to the first memorable smooch of my young life. I blissed out, again, and had to drag myself away from those sexy lips and back to the movie.

Thor has nuttin' on Matt, I gloated. I couldn't wait to tell Amaya, and briefly plotted flashing there with Matt for a short pitstop on our way home.

We managed to keep our lips to ourselves for the rest of the movie, but his hand remained firmly in mine—between bouts of snacking and the inevitable bathroom break, that is.

I wished the movie would go on forever, but eventually the ending credits forced me back to reality and the realization that all good things really do come to an end.

"We gotta stay till the very, very last second," I explained to Matt, staying put in my chair but powering the recliner back into a sitting position. "Marvel always puts sneaky

THE CURSE OF CUR

extra stuff way at the end when most people have given up and left the theatre."

Over half of the seats had emptied of those novices who didn't know any better or the impatient peeps who would google it when they got home, but we had to stick it out—it was a rule, after all.

I was in dire need of another pit stop from all the soda, though, so as soon as the truly final finale was over (and a disappointing 30-second nothingburger it was), I raced from the theatre and into the nearest bathroom. As I washed my hands, I looked up to admire the new silver hoop earrings Mom had bought me for Christmas, and noticed one of them had gone missing.

No! I just got those, and they were already my favs. *WTH.*

Knowing the theatre was probably empty by now, I rushed to the nearest stall and flashed from there to the back row where we'd been sitting, frantically hoping it had fallen down into the cracks of my seat.

I was so engrossed in my search that I didn't hear anyone come in, and felt a light tap on my shoulder. Assuming it was Matt, I turned to tell him about losing my earring, but I was instead confronted with a stranger. I juked back in surprise.

The man was handsome, even though blondes with blue eyes weren't really my thing—but it was his smile and the foreign accent that immediately threw me for a loop.

"Is your name Baylee?" he asked, as he held up my earring. "And could this be what you're looking for?"

Now I was confused, and my gut was going crazy. *Yeah, where were you three minutes ago?*

"How do you know my name, and why do you have my earring?" I demanded, reaching for it, but he pulled it back

192

and held it aloft.

"Just come with me nice and quiet, and all your questions will be answered."

Suddenly my eyes widened as reality dawned on me. *Holy snarkies, the FFNN!* Was this The Scion? He wasn't dressed as a minion, he was dressed like a young hipster. And he hadn't immediately attacked me, throwing me further into confusion.

But I knew I was dead Redeemer meat if I went anywhere with him, and I looked around, trying not to panic. I threw out a mental tether to Matt. "Matt, where are you? I need you!" But the connection was immediately shut down, something I didn't know if anyone else could do from within Matt's mind. Was it Matt himself who'd disconnected?

"Dad!" I screamed through our bond, "help!" As I did so, I flashed behind the man and lunged for my earring, but he zipped to the other side of the room, laughing and taunting me.

I was not about to start a brawl with The Scion or one of his minions over an earring, and I was worried about Matt. I decided to flash myself to the mall food court—where there would be lots of people—while I waited for Dad.

Suddenly I felt a zap from behind, and everything faded to darkness. As I went down, only one question flashed through my mind:

Was Matt taken, too, or was he involved in my abduction?

Epilogue: Perrin

I awoke to a bad taste in my mouth and a pounding headache. *What, for the love of squirrels and chipmunks, happened to me?*

I rubbed my head and tried to stand, but was stopped by a tether just like I'd seen on Dad for years—on his warriors, too. I was trussed up to the wall, my upper body lolling to the side. I unsteadily pushed myself into a sitting position and leaned against the wooden paneling, peering around the darkened room.

I was alone, that much was obvious. But for how long?

I raised a hand to my neck and felt the control collar that was the signature move of our enemies, a rising horror enveloping me. *Well played, Scion.*

I was in the deepest of doodies now, and I had no idea how I was gonna crawl out of it.

Most importantly, I wasn't in Kansas anymore.

Or even in Culpeper, of that I was sure. There was a part of me that just knew, without any obvious signs to indicate its truth, that I was on Perrin.

The word *home* lodged in my gut.

I tried to throw a mental tether out to Dad, hoping against hope that he could sense me and would answer. But I was greeted only by the slosh of my heart against my ribcage, and a very real fear twisting its way through my entrails.

I'm on my own.

We hope you enjoyed Tamira Thayne's
The Curse of Cur.

**COULD YOU TAKE A MOMENT TO GIVE THE BOOK
A SHORT REVIEW ON AMAZON.COM? YOUR REVIEWS
MEAN THE WORLD TO OUR AUTHORS, AND HELP THEM
EXPAND THEIR AUDIENCE AND THEIR VOICE.
THANK YOU SO MUCH!**

*Find links to The Curse of Cur and all our great books
on Amazon or at www.whochainsyou.com.*

About the
Author

Tamira Thayne pioneered the anti-tethering move-ment in America, forming and leading the nonprofit Dogs Deserve Better for 13 years.

During her time on the front lines of animal activism and rescue she took on plenty of bad guys (often failing miserably); her swan song culminated in the purchase and transformation of Michael Vick's dogfighting compound to a chained-dog rescue and rehabilitation center. She's spent 878 hours chained to a doghouse on behalf of the voiceless in front of state capitol buildings nationwide, and worked with her daughter to take on a school system's cat dissection program, garnering over 100,000 signatures against the practice.

She's the author of the Chained Gods series, the Animal Protectors Series, *Foster Doggie Insanity* and *Capitol in Chains*. She's the editor of *More Rescue Smiles*, and the co-editor of *Unchain My Heart* and *Rescue Smiles*.

In 2016 she founded Who Chains You, publishing books by and for animal activists and rescuers.

Also from Tamira Thayne

THE KNIGHTS CHAIN:
A CHAINED GODS SERIES STORY

The Akita was massive, a fine example of the breed—with the single exception of his current physical state: skeletal, matted, and attached to a cement post by a thick logging chain. He refused to let those things bother him, however; they were mere nuisances, after all.

What mattered most to him was that any of his captors—the men in black—who crossed his path would die.

Simple as that.

He was done with the torture, had enough of the domination. His mind may have been jumbled, with memories of the past escaping him—but he knew one thing for sure: he was more than this beast on a chain. For now, he would wait...

The Knight's Chain, a short story, precedes *The Curse of Cur*, and can be read before Book 2 of The Chained Gods Series or after to flesh out the character of the Knight.....*Read more and order from whochainsyou.com, Amazon, and other outlets.*

Also from Tamira Thayne

FOSTER DOGGIE INSANITY: TIPS AND TALES TO KEEP YOUR KOOL AS A DOGGIE FOSTER PARENT

Have you ever fostered a dog—happy to make a difference—but wondered why you felt frustrated and alone in your experience? Do you want to foster a dog, but don't know where to start, how to prepare, and what to expect? Have you experienced burnout or compassion fatigue in your rescue experience? If so, this is the book for you. Described as "an embrace from a friend who understands what we all go through; it is a beacon of hope to let other rescuers know they are not alone—a must-read for anyone involved in rescue."

This is not a book about dog training, but a book about people training while working with dogs...*Read more and order from whochainsyou.com, Amazon, and other outlets.*

Also from Tamira Thayne

MORE RESCUE SMILES: BEST-LOVED ANIMAL TALES OF RESILIENCE & REDEMPTION

The heart of the animal rescue world lies in its stories—of freedom, of love, and of sacrifice by those who not only acknowledge but embrace the human-animal bond and its wondrous gifts.

In our second rescue story compilation, Who Chains You Books is pleased to share a glimpse into the emotional lives of animal rescuers and the living beings they hold close. Join us for another helping of heartwarming anecdotes, as Clancy triumphs, Tallulah escapes, Alex survives, and a host of other animals steal our hearts.

Through these stories, you'll get a behind-the-scenes look into the relationships between rescuers and not only dogs and cats, but horses, cows, pigs, birds, and even a ferret, in this delightful second installment of *Rescue Smiles*.

We hope you're as captivated by the kinship between human and animal as we are . . .*Read more and order from who-chainsyou.com, Amazon, and other outlets.*

About Who Chains You Books

WELCOME TO WHO CHAINS YOU: PUBLISHING AND SPIRITUAL MENTORING FOR ANIMAL ACTIVISTS AND ANIMAL RESCUERS.

Who Chains You Publishing brings the work of animal activists and rescuers to your doorstep through books highlighting successes, missteps, and the brightest imaginative endeavors of those who love animals and fight on their behalf.

Animal activists and rescuers find ourselves at the forefront of THE social issue of modern times. The last hundred years have seen major leaps for women's rights, racial equality, and—most recently—gay rights. Even the animals have gained some ground. But, unfortunately, we have a LONG way to go for true freedom for those who remain voiceless in our society.

We hope you'll visit our website and join us on this adventure we call animal advocacy publishing. We welcome you.

Read more about us at whochainsyou.com.

www.ingramcontent.com/pod-product-compliance
Lightning Source LLC
Chambersburg PA
CBHW072103170626
46813CB00004B/1441